Tucker McBride

Just Blew In

Doris Gaines Rapp

Tucker McBride Just Blew In

Doris Gaines Rapp

Daniel's House Publishing

Huntington, Indiana

In Cooperation with

Never Alone Publishing

Fort Wayne, Indiana

Copyright 2026 Doris Gaines Rapp
Huntington, Indiana 46750

This book is a work of historic/biographic fiction. Some characters and incidents are products of the author's imagination and are used fictitiously. Conversations were created out of the author's imagination. The timeline of the actual events is compressed.

All rights reserved. No part of this book may be used or reproduced in any form or by any electronic or mechanical means, including information storage and retrieval systems, without permission in writing from the author, except a reviewer who may quote brief passages in a review.

Cover design is an Image by Clker-Free-Vector-Images from Pixabay. Help to place with the guidance of @Debi Lindhorst/The Type Galley. Other images are from the internet.

Scripture taken from the New King James Version®. Copyright © 1982 by Thomas Nelson. Used by permission. All rights reserved.

Library of Congress Control Number: 2026900109

ISBN-13: 979-8-9885283-9-5 **(paperback)**
ISBN-13: 979-8-218-90686-3 **(eBook)**

Warning
Tucker McBride rarely thinks before he acts. Learn from Tucker. Do not try Tucker's stunts.

Glossary
For an unfamiliar word with an asterisk (*) beside it, go to the back of the book for a definition or picture.

Dedication

This book is dedicated to all those who were injured, or lost their lives, in the Palm Sunday tornadoes of April, 1965. The outbreak of deadly twisters hit at least eighteen counties in Indiana. The greatest destruction was in the counties of St. Joseph, Elkhart (Dunlap) and LaGrange. The twisters also hit Howard County (Kokomo). Grant (Marion), and Adams (Berne) with a total of 137 deaths and vast damage to property across Indiana.

Dunlap was hit the hardest with 84 deaths and the destruction of Sunnyside, a complete housing area, and the Midway Trailer Park. Our home was missed by two blocks. Those who lived in the area will carry those memories all their live.

Acknowledgments

I recognize my writers group, Soli deo Gloria (to God be the Glory), for their positive encouragement and their great faith.

A big thank you to Vicki Borgman for the time and effort she put into editing. Since Tucker is really her dad, Bill Rapp, she is as familiar as I with all his antics.

Thank you, Debi Lindhorst, of The Type Galley in Warren, Indiana, for being able to help with the cover, even though she has retired.

Thank you to Kim Autrey, my publisher, editor, and friend. We are all blessed by your experience and dedication.

Thanks and many blessings to all my readers and fans of Tucker. Your enthusiasm and joy of reading Tucker McBride books, prompts each new edition.

Preface

The historic events that happened in this novel, my sixth Tucker McBride book, did not happen in Tucker's time, 1948. You can read about that day that occurred several years later, in history books and periodicals. My husband and I lived through it at the time it occurred. The happenings etched a memory in my mind and the thoughts of all those affected, that will remain forever. I have chosen to tell you about them through the eyes of fourteen-year-old Tucker McBride, the character modeled after my husband, Bill Rapp, who lived in Dunlap, in the big white house on the corner.

Contents

Preface		9
Chapter 1	Friday, March 19, 1948	15
Chapter 2	After School Friday	23
Chapter 3	Tucker Put it Together	30
Chapter 4	Snack Time in the Tepee	39
Chapter 5	Who Volunteered	43
Chapter 6	Saturday, the Day Before	48
Chapter 7	Off to Throw a Pot	55
Chapter 8	Sing a Story of the Old West	62
Chapter 9	Sowing the Seed	67
Chapter 10	A Drive and a Motor	71
Chapter 11	Up Alone	75
Chapter 12	Palm Sunday	80
Chapter 13	The Class	88
Chapter 14	A Family Gathering	93

Chapter 15	A Slight Correction	99
Chapter 16	Sunday Afternoon	101
Chapter 17	Another Tornado	111
Chapter 18	Sunnyside	117
Chapter 19	Helping Harvey	124
Chapter 20	Joe to the Rescue	131
Chapter 21	The Teapot	135
Chapter 22	Safe in the Bathtub	139
Chapter 23	Adam's Crayons	146
Chapter 24	Checking In	153
Chapter 25	The Entertainer	157
Chapter 26	Going Home	166
Chapter 27	The Morning After	170
Chapter 28	Life Needs Reassurance Sometimes	174
Chapter 29	Where is Micky?	180
Chapter 30	Joe Helped	184
Chapter 31	A Short Stop	191
Chapter 32	Checking on the Family	195

Chapter 33	Who is Coming?	201
Chapter 34	Come Fly With Me	208
Chapter 35	Slapstick	216
Chapter 36	Another Idea	222
Chapter 37	An Egg Hunt	226
Chapter 38	Easter Sunday	230
Afterword		236
Glossary		238
Recipes		240

Chapter One
FRIDAY, MARCH 19, 1948

Tucker couldn't believe how fast the school's hallways emptied on March 19. It was Friday, only a few minutes after the final bell clanged that started the Easter break, between Palm Sunday and Easter. Classrooms were empty, as teachers stood at their doors, arms folded, seeming to ready themselves for a great escape. No one hung around. Those who hurried through the hall appeared empty-handed, their text books stashed in their lockers. They were all headed for the exits, their coats thrown over their arms. They were ready for the week of vacation. A whole week, to relax, travel to see grandparents, and have fun. Gramma's familiar words[1] sang in his head:

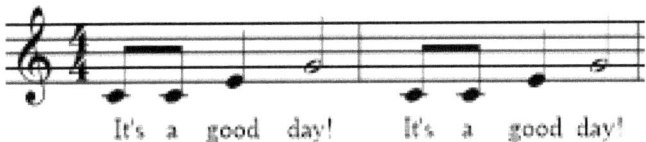

Thank you God, for a-no-ther good day!

Tucker slipped a little on some loose papers with bright red grades posted in the upper corner that lay on the floor. Someone, in their hurry to leave the building, had dropped a great fountain pen on the floor, like the ones required for Mrs. Swartzentruber's English class. A fuzzy white rabbit's foot with a locker key attached, and various other items of possible value to the owner lay strewn on the hardwood floor.

Mr. Weaver was already pushing his wide dust mop, covered with a lemon oil-soaked towel, down the hall. To the janitor's way of thinking, if it was on the floor, it was trash. And, as long as he was going to have to push the huge mop down every hall in the school, he might as well polish the floor a little as he walked. Mr. Weaver and his staff weren't going to dilly-dally around. Apparently, they wanted to get home and begin Easter break as soon as possible like everyone else.

Walking in a near-run past Mrs. Funderbird's room, Tucker smelled the rank odor of a smashed hardboiled egg. It probably fell from someone's lunch box and rolled over near the wall. He scooped up the rabbit's foot keyring and the sticky pen, wiped the pen on his jeans, and carried them into the school office before the super-mops got to them.

Principal Dillard and Vice Principal Saltsburg were standing behind the glass-top counter, under a large framed poster of Saint Francis's prayer.[2] It was the new translation and included a sentence important to Tucker. "Where there is error, let me bring truth."[2] Tucker especially liked that line. It was about mistakes, and he figured he had made many blunders along the way.

From where the two men stood, opposite the glass window facing the hall, they could see everything in the hall. With their hands covering their mouth, they whispered to each other, and appeared to be laughing.

Tucker stopped just inside the door. "I see you're both in here. That leaves no one to stalk the halls."

Principal Dillard smiled and nodded toward the outer hall. "It's called patrolling the halls, Tucker. We're staying out of the stampede. If we're needed, we'll put on our combat jackets and charge into the thick of it."

Tucker's eyes narrowed as he thought about the school leaders who were hiding behind the window facing the south hallway. Squinting, he wondered when Mr. Weaver would take the Windex bottle to the sugary hand-print in the lower corner of the glass.

"Yes, Sir. You can wave at the students from here," Tucker agreed. He had learned over his school career, that it was best to agree with teachers and administrators. Pulling the pen from his pocket, he handed it to Mr. Saltsburg. "I found this fountain pen on the floor. It looks like a Parker. That's a really good one. Someone will miss it when the break is over."

"Thank you, Tucker." Mr. Saltsburg took the pen and tucked it into the corner of the over-stuffed lost-

and-found drawer under the counter. A lace-trimmed handkerchief tried to escape from the erupting drawer. Saltsburg slammed it closed with considerable effort. "What are your plans for the free week?"

Tucker beamed mischievously. "I have a keen project that will take a while to finish. If you're driving around the neighborhood, slow down by our house and check our backyard."

Everyone in Dunlap knew where the Moyer house was. Tucker, his older brother, and two sisters had lived with their grandparents, Joseph and Rebecca Moyer, since Tucker was four months old. The large farm, once owned by Gramma's parents, was the very land that the elementary school, junior high, and the high school now sat on. Tucker said no more. He really wanted his project to be a surprise so his secret could burst forth unexpectedly on everyone who might pass. With excited energy, he was anxious to leave. "Gotta run."

"No running in the hall," Mr. Saltsburg said with a laugh.

As Tucker hurried out of the office, Mr. Dillard called after him, "You're not going to tell us about your mystery plan?"

"Nope," Tucker called over his shoulder. "Come and see."

"Come and see what?" Mr. Justine, Tucker's woodworking teacher, asked as he walked by. Justine was carrying a large, wooden box. To Tucker, it looked like it was made out of orange crate wood. A paper ad for Florida Oranges was still glued to the side. He thought he could smell the scent of the great southern citrus fruit wafting up from the wood.

Tucker was always curious. After seeing the crate, his curiosity rose. "What did you make, Mr. Justine?"

"The boys got a couple of rabbits for their 4-H project," Justine said as he winced, perhaps from what may have been a splinter from the crate.

"Your kids are always working on a project of some kind," Tucker said with a huge smile. "I like that."

Mr. Justine closed his eyes in agreement. "Just like you, Tucker. So, what will be your fancy creation?"

"Something really special," Tucker said, trotting backward toward the door. "Your boys, Jinx and Jason, would love to see it, too. Bring them by, this evening or tomorrow. You just live up on Woodington's farm. You could pop down any time."

Mr. Justine stopped in the middle of the hall, repositioned the bulky rabbit crate, and called after Tucker, "I just might do that." There was no real point in trying to keep up. Tucker always had somewhere to go, something to do, and the sooner the better.

Down the hall and around the corner toward the band room, Tucker could hear several blasts on a trumpet. He figured it was Freddie Cooper on his horn. Everyone knew how much he liked to play the thing. Or, at least let loose with a couple of loud notes.

"Hey, Cooper," Gus Guston yelled. "Cut it out with the horn."

"Unless you want to pick up the cold metal pieces off the floor," Morty shouted.

Ah, Morty and Gus are teasing Freddie for the umpty-teenth time. Couldn't they be just a little bit friendly like they were last month?

"Hey, McBride," Tucker's friend, Christy called out. "Wait up." She hurried along. If she didn't catch Tucker before he hit the school door, he would soon disappear down the sidewalk.

"Christy," he teased, "you are so slow."

"All right, McBride, no teasing. Your legs are longer than mine," she reminded him as she followed him out the door.

Out along the sidewalk, the March wind was gently blowing, carrying the fresh fragrance of spring. Although the trees hadn't started to show their green, there was the promise of pale green leaf buds popping out on the branches. Tucker closed his eyes and inhaled the clean air.

"You guys." Freddie Cooper moaned loudly as he pushed the door open behind Tucker and Christy. "Didn't you hear my horn. I need your help. You have to save me next week." He caught up to them at the point where the sidewalk ended at the side street, and the unpaved alley began on the other side of Kimmer Avenue.

Christy stopped and spun around, and her book bag wacked Freddie's arm. She grabbed his woolly tan jacket by both shoulders. "Save you from what? How can we help if we don't know what you're afraid of."

"I'm not afraid," Freddie denied as he hoisted his trumpet case up a little higher. It was bulky but beloved.

"It's not what," he gasped, out of breath.

"Then from who," she demanded. Freddie's jacket was crumpled in her hands.

"Okay." Tucker turned Freddie around and planted both feet in front of him. "We'll rescue you, as long as the threat isn't just in your mind. But, we'll save you …" he paused and glared into Freddie's eyes. "Again, from … whom?"

"My little cousin, Micky," Freddie whaled. "He's going to spend the whole week at our house. That's one hundred and sixty-eight hours. Micky's parents are going to California." He gasped for air as he seemed to process the inescapable event in his mind. "Micky will already be at my house by the time I get home. His parents said they would drop him off early, just as soon as Mom gets home from the grocery."

Then he paused and thought. "I wonder how much food he'll eat this week?" Continuing to gasp in air, he said, "He got out of his half-day kindergarten in Goshen at noon. Tucker, he'll be there by the time I get home, and he's only five … years … old."

"I'm sorry to hear he's staying at your house all week, Freddie," Tucker said with measured sympathy. "Even more sad, it's happening when you are supposed to have a week off, seven days to yourself, free from homework and classes," Tucker said with a calm, sympathetic tone. Shaking his head in sorrow, he added, "And, I'm really sorry he's only five years old."

"You're sorry he's five?" Christy sassed. "I can't believe you two smart-thinkers. He can't help being a kindergartener."

"I know. I know." With his right arm flapping and the left swinging the trumpet case, Freddie hurried down the alley ahead of Tucker. The deep gravel crackled under his feet. Zipping to the side of the alley, he put his hand on the cold wrought iron of Moyers' garden gate. He opened it for Tucker and huffed, "Mom will expect me to watch him all the time." He lowered his head, catching his breath. "Are you going to be at home this afternoon, or do you have to work?"

"Yep, I'll be home. Butch said he could handle the filling station by himself. He said he doesn't have any scheduled oil changes or new tires to mount. But I have a project to build," Tucker said as excitement mounted inside of him again, like giggles were bubbling in his stomach. "I might finish my plan today, but I'll still be enjoying it tomorrow, too. If you go home and bring Micky over, your little cousin can help with the plan. He'll have to help me build what I'm building, or stay out of the way."

"Thank you, thank you," Freddie blew out a sigh of relief. "I promise, Micky won't get in your way one time," he assured him. "He'll sit far away from whatever you're doing and watch." With prayerful hands, he said, "Bless you, bless you, my friend."

Tucker stepped past Freddie and popped through the gate and into the back of his yard near the sleeping garden. "Wait until you see what we're going to do. You will flip your wig." He blew into the yard like a whirl wind. "I'll change my clothes first, dive into the cookie crock, then I'll meet you in the backyard."

Chapter Two
AFTER SCHOOL FRIDAY

Tucker ran through the house, taking off his jacket as he moved. He could smell the pot of coffee in the kitchen that was always hot and ready for drinking. He flipped his coat over the back of a dining room chair, plopped his ball cap on the table, and kept going. His dark brown hair stuck out in as many ways as his cap had stirred it.

"Tucker!" Gramma called after him. "Hang up your jacket."

"I know, I know, Gramma," Tucker called over his shoulder as he hurried to the steps in the entry hall. "I'll get it in a minute. I'm going out again after I change my jeans." He got to the stairs and flew up, in his usual flight pattern, two treads at a time. A dark-blue flowered carpet runner, held to each tread by a silver, metal carpet rod, brightened the stairway. Every step was a well-rehearsed pattern of ascending to the second floor.

In his bedroom, he unlaced his shoes and kicked them into the corner. Then, he quicky peeled off his school jeans and hung them on a peg inside his closet.

Now, where are they? he muttered to himself. *Ah.* He saw something blue and pulled out a pair of everyday pants from halfway under his bed. They had a hole in the right knee, perfect for wearing while completing his project.

Now, where are my work shoes? Taking a fast visual sweep of his room, he spotted them between his chest of drawers and the wall. Grabbing his high-top clodhopper shoes, he plopped down on the edge of his bed, put the work shoes on, and laced them up. There was no time to waste. He had to begin his project before his excitement went off like fireworks and blew off the top of his head.

The stairs to the attic were strangely located in Tucker's bedroom closet. Excitedly, he jerked back his hanging clothes, and charged up the steps to the right of his dress pants, nearly falling over his feet. He knew exactly where it was. He had investigated the attic many times.

Tucker knew every inch of the house. He had lived in his grandparents' home since he was a baby. As Tucker grew from infancy into a fourteen-year-old, he had searched every closet, every drawer, and every inch of the attic.

This time, it was the package that Gramma's cousin, Sam Treadway, had ordered that had captured Tucker's imagination and wouldn't let go of its hold on him. Tucker had been fascinated by the package since it was delivered.

Moving several boxes out of the way, he grabbed some long, slick poles that had been stored under the eaves. Pulling and tugging, he drug them out into the center of the third-floor space. Then, he searched and retrieved a large, tan buffalo hide. The aroma of leather filled his nose like a perfume. Next, he opened the window that faced the backyard, and tossed the heavy, cap-like leather piece out the attic dormer. He figured that would be a shorter route to the ground than the stairs.

He knew the project was going to be amazing. It had to be. It was finally a dream come true. He was going to construct a Lakota-style tepee in his own backyard, even though a tepee in Indiana was unusual.

The Potawatomi and Miami tribes that originally settled in the Elkhart area didn't use tepees. Those Native Americans needed more solid structures to protect them from the Northern Indiana snowy winters with blowing ice, and the hot summers when temperatures could rise, like it did on August 27 of that year, to 96 degrees.

Tucker loved reading everything he could about the old west. Details of their lives and pictures of the mountains and prairies were all in Uncle Jacob's magazines that respectfully graced the many shelves in the dining room.

Uncle Jacob was a bachelor and still lived at home. As the children's legal guardian, he filled the house with books and periodicals. *National Geographic* magazines, several newspapers arrived every day, and the monthly *Reader's Digest* were but a few.

Tucker would select several issues of a magazine, with articles about the old west. Then he'd spread them out on the living room floor, plop down on his stomach with his long legs tucked under the couch so no one would trip over him, and devour everything *National Geographic* presented in their colorful layouts. On many Saturdays, Tucker sat in the darkened Elco Theater, with flickering lights from the cinema presenting the thundering hoofbeats of the western cowboys.

Sam had stored the tepee at the Moyer home many months before. He had it shipped back home to Indiana while he was traveling out west.

Tucker pranced with excitement the day a truck arrived with the huge carton and accompanying poles. He wanted to pull open the cardboard box before it hit the ground.

Tucker believed that putting something together or taking it apart, was the best way to spend an afternoon. So far, he had been successful at the putting objects back together. Tucker's intuition took over and guided his curious hands. Or maybe his young ability came from the many years he spent following Grandpop around the house and out into his workshop, that gave Tucker the insight into how things were made. Perhaps, those daily experiences were apprenticeship training for Tucker.

Grandpop had told Sam he could store the tepee in the attic until he and Sarah were married and were settled in their farmhouse. Since they were married last Christmas, Tucker knew Sam would come soon and claim his property.

He thought for a second about the best way to get the pieces to the yard. He decided the poles and one-piece outer covering would be much easier to get out of the attic if the large covering were removed from the enormous, square cardboard box.

The tepee was too small for a Lakota family to live in. It was an individual dwelling Sam had bought from Maria Garcia's tribe, the same Native American woman who had sold Sam her son's Chief's blanket after Dakota died in World War II.

Tucker's tepee adventure was in March, when Elkhart ordinarily had temperatures around a crisp 35 degrees. That year, there were higher than normal temperatures in the valleys of the rivers, as one of Uncle Jacob's books[3] noted, referring to the St. Joseph and Elkhart rivers. It was the warmest March on record, and it couldn't have come at a better time. The week off from school would be full of warm sun-shine and blue skies. He would take advantage of the warm weather and the short vacation by setting up Sam's tepee in the backyard. He had to test how it all went together. Anyone who knew Tucker would have known that.

Tucker's curiosity required that he tinker with the simplest to the most complicated things. He had taken the family's floor model radio apart when he was younger and put it back together. Grandpop had slipped into the kitchen and whispered in Gramma's ear, "How does that boy do it?"

Tucker thought for a moment, then came up with a clever idea. He carefully slid the tepee poles out the window and let them slither across the black shingles of the summer kitchen roof and onto the ground below. He quickly closed the window before his grandfather came up to investigate the cause of the crisp breeze that no doubt would have drifted down the stairway.

Tucker was fourteen and in the eighth grade. That made his grandfather ninety years old. Tucker didn't want his grandfather to climb the steps again or worry about a heat leak upstairs.

Retired from the New York Railroad many years ago, Grandpop was still the janitor at their red brick church across Moyer Avenue that ran beside their house. Occasionally, Grandpop would climb onto the slanted church roof to clean out the eaves, and Tucker was right beside him, helping in any way he could. But there was no need for Grandpop to rattle through the house just because Tucker was involved in one of his projects.

That adventurous Friday afternoon, as Tucker came downstairs and walked through the dining room on his way to the side door, Gramma spoke up. "What's all the noise about, Tucker? It sounded like you were dancing on the roof."

"No, Gramma." Tucker went into the kitchen and opened the cabinet where Gramma stored the old earthen-ware cookie crock. The shelf smelled like cinnamon and creamy butter. He reached into the crock and grabbed as many cookies as his fist could hold. He explained, "Sam said I could set up his tepee this spring. I shoved the poles and the covering out the window instead of using the steps to get them to the ground. That seemed smarter." Tucker removed his light weight jacket from the back of the dining room chair, put it on, zipped it up, shoved the sugar cookies into his pocket, and headed outside.

"Come on, Joe," he called to his dog. The old German shepherd followed Tucker outside just as the door banged shut. Tucker winced at the sound, knowing how it might have startled his grandmother. He smiled and had to admit, setting up the tepee had to be the most exciting thing he had done in a long time. He had been ready for months.

Chapter Three
TUCKER PUT IT TOGETHER

Out in the yard, Uncle Jacob had pulled the lawn mower out of the storage shed and was oiling the wheels when Tucker rounded the corner of the house. The push mower with extra-large wheels would be ready when spring greeted the fresh green grass.

Jacob was the eldest brother of Tucker's mother. He had never married, still lived with Gramma and Grandpop, and became the legal guardian of Tucker and his three older siblings. Since his father's grief kept him from caring for his four children, they were taken in by the Moyers. Gramma Moyer was sixty-six and their grandfather was seventy-six when they started raising a second family again. Now that Grandpop was growing older, Jacob's duties in the yard and garden increased.

"What is Sam's tepee doing on the ground?" Uncle Jacob closed and latched the shed door. The lock wasn't intended to keep the neighbors out. They wouldn't have thought to steal anything from Joseph Moyer. He loaned them every tool he owned. The brass latch kept the raccoons and mice out.

"I'm going to set it up," Tucker said as he gathered up the poles from where they had scattered when they landed in the yard. "Sam and Sarah are going to stop by after church on Sunday to see it all constructed again."

"You know, Elkhart, Indiana, is called the 'Trailer Capital of the World.' Are you going to start a tepee construction company and move up to mobile homes?" Uncle Jacob stooped to pick up a few of the poles and leaned on one like the wise man of Dunlap.

"Nope." Tucker laughed. "Just this one." Grabbing the buffalo hide by the corner, he dragged the heavy outer covering farther out into the yard, only guessing at which was the top and which the bottom. "I've seen this thing up in the attic for months. I had to set it up."

"Well, put it aways off from the garden." Uncle Jacob smiled a little, brushed dust from his pants, and headed toward the house. "We won't plant any warm-weather vegetables, like tomatoes and peppers, until early May. But the cold-hardy ones like broccoli and peas, we'll get in the ground by late March. We'll start tilling the ground soon."

"Okay, Uncle Jacob." Tucker thought about the earthy smell of plowed ground as he headed to Grandpop's work shed. "I going to put it over by the apple orchard, beside the grape arbor. We won't need to be in that part of the yard for months. I'll take the tepee down next weekend, before the school break is over."

"Um-hum," quiet and steady Uncle Jacob muttered as he opened the back door into the summer kitchen.

Tucker slipped inside Grandpop's small and packed work shed. Tools were lined up on the wall and organized by type and size, hammers, screw drivers, and such, and even filled some large chests with tools he had collected over the years. He reached for a heavy wooden hammer and a coiled length of Grandpop's handmade rope.

Grandpop had created the rope. Every day, the truck driver from the *Elkhart Truth* newspaper would drop off bundles of papers on the front steps of Winkler's Grocery Store, across the street. Grandpop arranged for the delivery to be changed to their house. Newsboys and girls met each day on Moyer's large front porch to fold their newspapers, out of any rain or snow. In exchange for that convenience, the newspaper boys and girls left the string that had tied each bundle of papers. Grandpop would braid the lengths into a longer, thicker rope.

"There," Tucker mumbled to himself. He was a talker, whether anyone was around or not. "That piece of rope will do," he assured himself. As he re-locked the door, his friend, Freddie Cooper, rode up on his Schwinn bicycle. The bike was like Tucker's deep maroon Schwinn with white stripes that his dad, Sean McBride, had given him two years before.

Sean had remarried twice after Tucker's mother died. He and his third wife and small son lived just a few miles from the Moyer's world on the corner in Dunlap.

"Freddie, so is this your little cousin?" Tucker asked as he lay the stiff coiled rope on the ground next to the tepee poles.

Freddie brushed some red hair from his forehead as he helped a small boy down off the bike's handlebars.

The boy plopped on the ground, strong and straight. He was as skinny as Freddie, with a similar shade of auburn hair. "Yeah, this is my cousin Micky that I told you about." Freddie watched as Tucker continued to size up the task at hand. "What are you doing? What is all of this?"

"It's my cousin Sam Treadway's tepee that he's had stored in our attic." Tucker picked up several of the poles and said, "Grab a few, Freddie. Have your little friend drag one, too."

"Little!?" the boy snapped back. "Shucks, I'm the tallest boy in my class. Who do you think you're talking to?"

"I'm talking to you, Mister," Tucker said as his eyes danced.

Freddie watched as the boy picked up the end of a tepee pole and began dragging it after him. "Micky is small but mighty. He helps real good."

"Great!" Tucker led the way out the fence gate and into the orchard area on the other side of the alley, where the dry, barren grape vines still climbed on the trellis. "Over here." He flopped the poles between the grape arbor and the cluster of apple trees, still in their winter sleep. "Let's go get the tepee cover."

Gramma's flock of chickens near the orchard clucked away and batted their wings from the roof of the coop. Some of the hens pranced around the small chicken yard, their soft feathers splayed out, letting everyone know that the tepee-building boys were in their space.

Joe laid down under an apple tree, stretched out, and watched the new happenings. The war dog ignored the noisy chickens. After all, his job was to watch and protect, not to be on poultry patrol.

Tucker picked up the heavy buffalo hide on one side and nodded at Micky to grab another corner. "You take that spot, and Freddie, you get the other end." Together, they moved the protective semicircular shell of the tepee onto the ground and spread it out.

"Sam said to tie the three longest poles together at the top. Micky, put your finger on the rope while I tie the knot." Once Tucker tied the three wooden poles from the aspen tree and tightly secured them with Grandpop's special rope, the boys raised them up to form a tripod. "Good, now Sam said to arrange the rest of the poles around the base of the tripod." Once Tucker had pointed to each place, Micky helped Freddie drag each aspen pole over to the outer edge to form a circle.

While the tepee began to take shape, Christy strolled confidently into the yard with her hands on her hips. She, too, had changed her clothes. Instead of the wool, pleated skirt and short sleeve sweater she had worn to school, she had put on jeans, like the boys wore, and a sweatshirt. Those jeans were stronger and more fitted for after-school projects, especially Tucker's kind of activity. "What are you guys doing?"

"Miss Christmas Tree has arrived, and spring is just creeping in," Tucker called out as he looked up from the scattered pile that would eventually become a tepee. "You're just in time."

She scowled, gritted her teeth, and hissed, "Call me Christy, Tucker McBride, or I'll leave."

"Oh, sorry, Miss Tree." He paused, gave a deep "Ahem," and said, "Christy!" He bowed and added, "You're here just in time. We could use your help with the outer covering of the tepee."

Christy batted her eyelashes and pantomimed the flutter of a paper fan. "I would be happy to lend some assistance to my friends." Then she stopped and looked closer. "Crackers, what are you making?"

Turning to Freddie, Tucker rolled his eyes. "Okay then." He walked around to the opposite side of the outer tepee covering that lay on the ground beside the pole structure. "Freddie, you take that corner where the painted border begins. And … Micky, you get ahold of that part down at the other corner. Christy, you stand inside the circle of poles and make sure they don't slip, so the hide lays smoothly draped around them.

"We are building a tepee, Christy. Sam told me, in Lakota communities, the young people learn how to assemble tepees and are taught that each pole represents a different virtue. I don't know which virtues they learned, but if they can put a tepee together, so can we."

"I've got it." Christy took her position inside the circle and looked from one pole to the next. "They look secure so far."

Tucker and Freddie draped the hide over the poles, like they were putting a large cape on a huge mannequin in Ziesel's Department Store window. Holding the hide in place, he asked, "Christy, there's a long leather bag over there by the apple tree. Would you please bring it here?"

She started to swoop it off the ground, then stopped as she secured the long wooden sticks that began to slide out of the bag. "What is this?"

"Sam called them lacing pins." Tucker held the front of the tepee closed and nodded toward the bag. "Okay, Christy. See the matching holes, like a pair of shoes? Rather than shoestrings, we're supposed to use the pins to lace the tent together. You put them through the holes that run from the door opening to the tepee poles at the top."

"That is amazing," Christy said with a giggle.

"Freddie, you get the top one if Christy can't reach it." Tucker continued at his post, holding it together until a lacing pin was inserted. After Freddie helped to push the last one through the two holes, lacing the top together, Tucker was ready for the last step. "Now we stake the lower edge to the ground." He handed the second bag of tent stakes to Micky. "Here, you carry them from one stake hole to the next." With the wooden hammer, Tucker pounded each stake through the grommeted hole at the hem of the covering and into the ground.

Joe watched each tap of the hammer. Tucker smiled. "I'll bet Joe remembers when he was with the K-9 Corps during the war. The tepee is a little like a G.I.'s tent."

In Tucker's mind, he could see the tepee standing like a proud dwelling on the western plain. He stood back, folded his arms, and smiled. He could almost feel the wind swooping down from the imaginary mountains he could see in his mind and blow the flap opening. It was together, and he felt good. He didn't think about the later task of taking the tepee down, and storing each lacing pin and tent stake in its proper leather bag. Putting-away was the task he was still working on … when he thought about it.

It had already started off to be the best vacation ever. He even had the next few days off from work at Butch Randolf's Sinclair filling station across the street. Butch told him to enjoy Saturday and Palm Sunday. He would be able to cover it all. He would see Tucker next week. Imagine, a weekend to do nothing.

Chapter Four
SNACK TIME IN THE TEPEE

Tucker stood back in amazement, beaming with pride. "It feels like, at any minute, Dakota Garcia will ride across the plain, with his Chief's blanket thrown across his horse's back."

"This is wunderbar." Gramma's eyes were wide as she walked across the grass, gripping the paper sack she carried tightly against her chest. At only 4 foot 10 ½ inches tall, the bag looked half as big as she. Her little silky terrier, Tiny, was at her heals.

Tucker's smile spread across his face. "It sure was fun building it. Come inside, Gramma."

Christy put her hand on Mrs. Moyer's shoulder and beamed. "I'm glad I came by when I did. I never thought I'd help put up a real tepee." She was so excited, she repeatedly brushed her blond hair from her eyes.

Tucker opened the entrance flap. "It's not a family-size dwelling, but we'll all fit inside, if some of us don't sit down."

Tiny yipped and twisted without stopping as Gramma got closer and surveyed the masterpiece of tepee building. Tiny squatted down, with her little paws out in front of her, and yipped until she bounced off the ground. The little dog seemed to be clear about evicting strange, large conical objects from her yard.

Gramma handed Tucker the paper bag. "Ja, gut, but I'm afraid I won't be sitting. I'd need all of you to get me down on the ground, and your grandpa's pully, fed up through the top of the tepee, and attached to the nearest apple tree, to haul me back up again."

"Gramma." Tucker sniffed at the bag. "What's in here?"

She stepped inside and twirled slowly, taking in every angle of the tepee her cousin, Sam, had lived in when he was on a Lakota reservation in western South Dakota. "It is amazing," she whispered. "Sam slept in this leather house in the icy cold winters and the blazing hot summers. Can you imagine it?" Pointing to the bag, she added, "I brought out some peanut butter sandwiches, with my homemade bread and grape preserves."

"Sandwiches?" Freddie jumped at the mention of food. He had been around Tucker's family for a long time and knew how thick Mrs. Moyer sliced her bread.

"You bet, ya," she said and opened the bag.

Tiny yipped and jumped repeatedly, until she landed in a heap on the ground of the tepee. Joe walked in lazily, opened his mouth, grabbed the little pest by the nap of the neck, and flung her out through the opening.

Tucker laughed and rubbed the top of his dog's head.

"Thanks, Joe. She was becoming a nuisance, wasn't she?"

Gramma stretched and arched her back. "I'm going back in and see if your grandpa has gotten up from his nap. He wants to go over to the church soon and make sure everything is ready for Sunday service. It's a special day, being Palm Sunday." She stopped and pointed at the sack. "Tucker, I know the sandwich won't hurt your appetite for dinner. But Christy, Freddie, you'll have to pace yourselves."

Freddie stared at the brown paper sack. "Yes, Ma'am. I'll eat slowly."

Gramma looked down at the frantic little animal. "Tiny, you little scamp. You come with me." She turned to walk back to the house, then she added, "I saw the young one ride up with Freddie." With her hand waving over her head, she shouted, "There's a sandwich in there for him, too."

"Thanks, Tucker's grandma." Micky bounced up and down on his heals and tried to reach the sack. "I'm Micky Cooper."

"Hi, Micky," she called over her shoulder and kept walking.

Tucker sat on the ground and pointed to a patch of grass where the other three could sit. They all sat cross-legged, Indian style, as Tucker passed out the wax paper wrapped sandwiches. As they bit into the crunchy peanut butter, and swooned over the sweet homemade grape preserves, silence fell inside the tepee as each delicious bite was savored.

As she enjoyed the gourmet PBJ, Christy wiggled and tried to tuck her jacket under her. "Wow, this ground is cold. If I'd known I'd be sitting on the earth itself, I would have worn a longer coat. I thought spring was on the way."

Tucker looked at the sky that was visible in the distance beyond the tepee opening. There was something different about it, but he didn't know what. He had never seen the sky like that before.

Chapter Five
WHO VOLUNTEERED?

"Hey, anybody in there?" a voice called from outside the tepee before Tucker could respond to Chrity's cold seat complaints.

"Yep, we're in here." Tucker swallowed a large nutty bite and looked out into the sunshine.

Pastor Daily bent down so he could see inside. "Tucker? Who is in there?"

"It's me, Pastor," Christy replied. "And Freddie Cooper and his little cousin, too."

"Little?" Micky bellowed from the hollow inside. He wiped his peanut butter mouth on his sleeve. "Hey, you guys, knock it off."

"Sorry, Micky," she called over his protests and chomped down on another bite of Skippy's best nut butter.

"Look at this, Gus," Morty said as he approached the tepee. "Who knew we would find a tribe of American Indians in Tucker's back yard? This is keen."

"Morty?" Tucker asked and swallowed hard. He had never heard Morty say anything very positive to him, or about him. He couldn't believe that Morty actually liked their work on the tepee. He had to admit, Morty and Gus did help last month.

"Hi, boys," Pastor Daily said as the two, known by everyone around Dunlap as the neighborhood bullies, came over to the portable dwelling.

"Tucker, where did you get this tepee?" Morty continued as he bent and looked inside. "This is swell."

Gus carefully moved around Pastor Daily and got closer. He ran his fingers over the soft, thick hide, and gently touched the lacing pins. "It's super."

Tucker's eyebrows arched. What had gotten into Gus and Morty? Tucker had to admit that he had talked to the two more at school since they stepped in and helped around Valentine's day. Was that it? Had the guys' behavior changed because Tucker had warmed up to them. But, wait. Those two misfits had bullied his friend, Freddie, for years. Tucker couldn't just be Mr. Nice-guy to those two after all they had done.

Tucker knew that Gramma would have had a different attitude. Originally, there were three in the bull trio. She had challenged the third one, Vinny Wagoner, to come to church. Challenge would be a polite term. She had influenced his change in Sabbath morning activity by telling him she would tell his father about his stalking the boys and bullying them. Vinny started coming to church and liked it. He was in the sanctuary every Sunday morning. Maybe kindness does change people.

"I came over to see Tucker," Pastor Daily began his explanation. "But, I'm glad you are all here." He sat down on the ground just outside the tepee and patted the fresh grass beside him. "Gus, you and your friend come and join me."

Morty watched as Gus joined the minister without so much as a smart aleck wisecrack. "You know Gus, do ya?"

Pastor Daily reached over and patted Gus on the shoulder. "Gus? Sure, of course I know him. Well, a little. His mother, Nancy Guston, comes to Bible study every Wednesday and to worship every Sunday morning."

Morty opened his mouth to speak, then stopped and sat down. He appeared to be brain smacked.

Pastor Daily continued, "Raymond Swartz was supposed to read the scripture Sunday during the service. His wife called to say that Raymond's father was in a car accident this morning, and Ray has gone to Michigan to be with his dad today and tomorrow, until his mom gets home from Alabama on Sunday night."

"I don't know Ray's dad, but, I hope he's okay," Tucker sympathized.

The pastor smiled. "He will be. He has a broken leg and doesn't get around very well, yet." The pastor adjusted his position on the ground, rubbed his leg, and appeared to shake off a leg cramp. "So ... I was hoping that one of you would read the morning Bible passage on Palm Sunday."

Silence fell over everyone in the tepee and those outside. No one even made eye contact with Pastor Daily. They all stared at the ground and seemed to be counting every blade of grass in their small spot of the yard.

"You mean, at the church over there?" Micky pointed to Tucker's church across the side road. "The church with the leaning steeple."

"The steeple doesn't lean, Micky," Freddie corrected him. "See, look again."

Micky frowned and checked the steeple one more time. "Yes, it does. Look at it."

The pastor smiled, and explained to Micky, "Since you are shorter than your cousin, you're physically closer to the bottom of the steeple. So, when you look up, it's at a more extreme angle than it is for a taller person. It could look like the tower is leaning to you."

"Hum," Micky began, "okay. But ... it's not because I'm short. I'm the tallest five-year-old in all of Goshen. And, the tower is still leaning."

Suddenly, Tucker became excited as he quickly jumped to his feet and popped out of the tepee. "Hey, I have a great idea."

"Okay," Pastor Daily drew out slowly. "Let's have it. I am listening."

Tucker pointed with enthusiasm. "Gus could read the scripture in church on Sunday. His mom is always there, and his dad comes as often as possible, with work and all."

"What?" Gus nearly choked on his sweet, fruity tasting Bazooka bubble gum. "Me?"

"Well ..." Morty began to stammer. "Gus and I have plans Sunday morning. We're already booked up. Sorry, Pastor Daily."

Tucker's mouth flew open. "Tomorrow morning? Morty, both you and Gus aren't seen around Dunlap on Sundays until mid-afternoon. You two must sleep until at least noon."

"Yeah, but ... but," Morty stuttered and sputtered. "Gus, say something!"

"I'll do it," Gus said quickly, softly. "I've been talking to Mrs. Harrison, the speech coach, about joining the high school debate team next year, and participate in the speech contests. And ..."

Morty blurted out. "Speech contests? Debating? You, Gus?"

Gus squared his shoulders and stood up straighter. "Why not me?" Defiantly, he stared at Morty while answering the pastor. "Sure, Pastor Daily, I would like to read from the Bible Sunday morning. It will be a great opportunity for me to begin to be in front of people."

Tucker would never have guessed that Gus would agree to stand up in front of the church and read. Everyone's eyes and ears would be on him. Maybe he didn't really know Gus at all.

Chapter Six
SATURDAY, THE DAY BEFORE

Tucker slept in until seven-thirty that Saturday morning, the day before Palm Sunday. It felt good. It had been a long time since he didn't have to get up early for something. He sat up, stretched, and looked out the window for any evidence of the coming spring. When he finally got downstairs, Gramma was walking through the dining room with her Bible.

"Well, good morning, Sleepy. Freddie just called. He wants you to call him back." She kept going and sat down by the window in the living room. It was her usual spot. The light from the bright sky helped her read, and the rocking chair fit her petite size.

"Thanks, Gramma." Tucker removed the receiver from the wall-hanging telephone and cranked in one short, two long, and two short cranks. He leaned into the mouth piece. "Hi, Freddie. Gramma said you called."

"Right," Freddie answered. "Believe it or not, the Easter Bunny is going to be at Winkler's Grocery this morning, in the dime store section. Mom wants me to take Micky." His voice was desperate, as it seemed to sound most of the time since yesterday. "Will you walk over with us? I don't want anyone to see us and think that I want to see the silly rabbit."

"The Easter Bunny? What time? I just got up." Tucker thought about his crispy breakfast cereal of Cornflakes and how hungry he was.

"Mom stopped in for milk last evening before they closed. Simon Winkler told her that the furry visitor will be there this morning at nine," Freddie said with a deep sigh. "He'll be there a few hours, but Tucker, I want to get this humiliation over as soon as possible."

Tucker laughed. "I can hear how much you really want to do this. Sure, I'll walk you two over."

Tucker wolfed down a small mixing bowl full of cereal. The crisp, toasted corn flavor always made him smile. He washed and dried the bowl, then replaced it on the cabinet shelf that Gramma had lined with newspaper.

After brushing his teeth, he came out of the bathroom. "Gramma, I'm going over to the grocery with Freddie pretty soon. He's taking Micky to see the Easter Bunny. Is there anything you need while I'm there?"

"The Easter Bunny?" Gramma gulped. "Easter has nothing to do with small animals with long ears. It is about our risen Savior."

Tucker knew his grandmother was right. He had gone to church since he was born and knew about the stone that was rolled away. He knew that Jesus had gone through all His agony for him and for everyone. But, he also knew that kids like the Easter Bunny. "It would have been better if they had called the white fuzzy one, the spring Bunny. I think it celebrates the welcoming of spring, and all the new little bunnies, chirping chicks in the nests, calves, colts, you know. When everything is new again."

"Tucker," Gramma called after him as he ran upstairs to get his shoes. "You are a smart boy."

"Thanks, Gramma," he shouted from the landing near the top of the stairs. He scrambled around in the bottom of his closet and pulled out his tan leather, ankle high boots, and prepared for another flight down the steps. Minutes later, Freddie knocked on the door.

"I'm leaving, Gramma," he shouted into the house as he closed the door.

Tucker, Freddie, and Micky walked along the grass up to the highway and stopped. The morning was glorious, with fluffy clouds in the bluest sky. Maybe it would be a great day after all. It was still early enough that not many cars passed.

"Pontiac!" Freddie shouted and pointed to a 1941 Pontiac Torpedo in bright red.

Tucker laughed and pointed out a white, four door car. "Hudson Terraplane," he shouted back "With the war over by almost two years, the car companies are going to make different models of sedans and other styles, and more brands should appear. We're going to have to learn the make and model of many more shiny new cars."

After looking both ways, with Tucker on one side and Freddie on the other, they hurried Micky across the road.

Inside the grocery, customers seemed to be buying the last-minute items needed for a family Palm Sunday dinner. Cans of sweet potatoes for candying in the oven, cartons of butter, and sliced pineapple for the top of the ham, were just a few of the items Tucker saw loaded in carts. But he couldn't stop. Micky had him by the hand and was dragging him through the store into the five-and-dime side of the business.

School supplies, white athletic socks, picture frames, and toys were just a few of the types of merchandise offered on the right side of the store. Fred Arbaugh sat on a high-backed chair Simon must have brought from home.

The Easter Bunny was positioned in front of the window where he could be seen both inside the store and out. Tucker had never seen a chair like that around the store, and he had even helped do some repairs in the store's attic.

"Hi, Fred," Tucker greeted.

Fred shook his head. "How did you know it was me?"

"Your shoes, Fred." Tucker pointed to a spot on Fred's high-top Converse tennis shoes. "You spilled that chocolate shake on your pants and shoes in the Olympia Candy Kitchen in Goshen the other day. I was there at the time. Looks like it stained the canvas."

"It did," Fred agreed, then looked at Micky. "Did you know that the Easter Bunny likes chocolate milk shakes?"

"No," Micky answered with a crooked smile. "I thought you'd like lettuce and carrots. Peter Rabbit did. He was always chased out of Mr. McGregor's garden."

"I do like vegetables," Fred Bunny admitted. With a big smile behind the bunny head piece, he asked, "I'm here to find out what kind of candy you would like in your Easter basket."

"It's not one kind," Micky said excitedly. "I like chocolate eggs, tons of jelly beans, and some Babe Ruth candy bars," he listed, numbering them from one finger to the next.

"Three kinds?" Fred's mouth opened wide in amazement. "Well, since you're a friend of Tucker's," he said as he took the note packet from his costume pocket, "I'll write down all of them. Then, before you leave, you take this note to Mr. Winkler, and he'll give you one of each."

"Wait," Freddie cautioned and positioned the Kodak Brownie No.2 Model F camera[4] to take a picture of Micky and the Easter Bunny. "Mom wants me to get a picture or two with her camera."

Micky smiled, then clowned around with a silly expressions. He jumped up and down and took the note as a few other children lined up to greet the Easter Bunny. "Where's Mr. Winkler, Freddie?"

"Over on the other side of the store," Freddie said, and allowed himself to be pulled over to the grocery, pretending a great deal of resistance.

Tucker stayed back to check out the athletic socks. Gramma could only darn his socks so many times before they just had to be replaced. He had his own money from his work at Butch's station and often bought the things he needed. He selected three pair of white gym socks. At ninety-eight cents a pair, that would be $2.94. Since Indiana didn't have any sales tax in 1948, three dollars would cover it.

"Hi, Tucker," cousin Sarah, Sam's wife, greeted as he sorted through the sock display. "I just stopped in to see what all the activity was about."

Tucker pointed to the white costumed character with long ears. "The Easter Bunny has arrived a week early."

"I came in for baking stuff. Your grandmother invited Sam and I to join the family for dinner after church tomorrow. I made two pies this morning and used up all the flour. Since I was next door, getting gas for the car, I thought I would stop in and pick up another five pounds. The pies are cooling on the counter."

"What kind?" Tucker loved pie. For the most part, it didn't matter what kind it was. He'd eat them all.

"Two cherry pies. I put up about twenty pint-jars of cherries from the trees in our backyard."

"Sounds great." Tucker swooned.

"After lunch today, Sam and I are going to throw some pots. Maria Garcia taught him how to make pottery when he lived out west. If you and Christy want to come out and make a bowl, that would be great." She saw Freddie corralling Micky who was carrying a paper sack. "I think Freddie needs a break. If he can find someone else to watch the boy, he can come, too."

"Wow!" Tucker thought out loud. "A real Indian pot. A Lakota tepee, now a Native American style pot. What a vacation!"

Chapter Seven
OFF TO THROW A POT

Christy almost bounced along as she sat squeezed between Tucker and Freddie in Tucker's Ford Model A. "I am so excited!" she squealed. "I can't wait to get there. Thank you for inviting me, Tucker."

"Sure," Tucker agreed as he shifted gears at the corner. "I thought you would like it. You like all that artsy stuff."

"Me too," Freddie echoed. "I get to spend a few hours away from Micky. He's a good kid, but he talks all the time."

"This has been the best vacation ever." Tucker pounded the shift knob. "I can't believe it. We put up a tepee Friday after school, and now we're going to make pottery. I never dreamed I'd actually make something out of clay."

"There's something else," Christy whispered, like it was her very own secret. "*The Westward Trail* is playing at the theater. Maybe we could all go after dinner. Freddie, that would give you more time away from Micky. Or, if you want to, you could bring him, too. It stars the Singing Cowboy."

"Yeah, Freddie." Tucker dodged a squirrel that ran in front of the car. "Bring Micky. He did a good job helping with the tepee." Then he thought a minute. "The only thing is, there isn't room for four in this seat."

Freddie laughed. "If Mom says he can come with us, I'll bring a blanket. Micky and I can sit in the rumble seat. I happen to like the rumble seat. If there was enough room, I'd ask Anna Fredrick if she'd like to come, too."

Christy patted his knee. "You are a brave young man, Freddie. With Micky, and Miss Woe."

"Okay, Christy," he protested, "she doesn't say, 'Woe is me,' as much as she used to."

"I'm sorry." She smiled through a rather weak apology. "You're right."

"Okay," Tucker gave in. "If Micky and Anna can come with us, I'll ask Uncle Jacob if we can use his car."

"Oh, wow!" Freddie cheered. "Thanks."

Tucker drove along County Road 13, out into the farmland of the township. He passed Whistler's Meat Packing Company on the left, and smiled. He and Betsy used to walk the mile and a quarter out to the plant to watch them slaughter pork and beef. Then the butchers would cut the meat into the familiar shapes of pork chops and steaks. Uncle Jacob would pick up some meat from Whistler's from time to time. Tucker could almost taste the lean, browned hamburgers from the grill in the backyard.

On the right side of the road, they soon passed the Jacobson farm. Willard and Janice Jacobson had lived there for forty years. Tucker often went out to their farm to play with their grandson when he was younger. He and Tim would climb the rough, wooden slats on the inside of the barn up to the hay loft. The hay smelled sweet and earthy. From there, they would grab the thick rope that hauled bales of hay up and into the loft above. Then, he and Tim would have great fun swinging by the rope and landing in a pile of fresh straw on the main floor of the barn.

When they arrived at the Treadway farm, Tucker pulled the black coupe into the driveway, beside the small cinder block milk house. He was so excited, he fumbled with his car key and dropped it as he stepped out of the car. Sam and Sarah's dog Fritz came over and sniffed out the key from where it had landed under the edge of the car.

Tucker scratched the dog behind his ears. "Thanks, Fritz." As he rubbed the dog vigorously, the sweet perfume of hay drifted up. "Fritz, you've been sleeping in the barn. I recognize the warm smell of hay."

Christy was finally able to straighten her right leg once Freddie got out. Pealing herself out of the cab, she bent over, then stood up and stretched. As Tucker stepped onto the side porch and knocked on the door, she was right behind him. Bric-a-brac hung from the edge of the roof and decorated the porch in the Victorian style.

Sarah opened the door, smiled, and gestured vigorously. "Come on in. This will be fun."

"Come in Tucker and all," Sam called from inside the pale green clapboard covered farm house.

The whole house smelled like luscious, yeasty, cinnamon rolls. Tucker could smell the yumminess as soon as he set one foot inside.

Sam was standing at the kitchen counter over a giant wooden bowl. The earthy container looked to be old. Not the kind of old that looked like it would break. The other kind of old, like it held history in every fiber.

"You're just in time," Sam said with a broad smile. "I was just going to mix the clay." He stopped over the bowl with a pitcher of water. "Tucker, Sarah drove slowly by your house and saw the tepee. She said it was magnificent! I haven't seen it. I was tilling the south field this morning and wasn't with her. I can't wait to see it tomorrow."

Tucker gave a wide grin. "It is pretty keen."

Sam put the water pitcher down and gave Tucker a side hug and laughed. "I bet it's keener than keen."

Tucker smiled a big smile. "It is keener than keen." The process of pot making that Sam had already put in place was stretched out in front of them. "Did you get the clay from here on the farm?"

"No." Sam slowly poured water onto a large mound of super dirt, fine powder-like clay. "Maria Garcie sent a big box of clay. I picked it up at the train station in Elkhart last week."

Christy watched the mixing process with wide eyes. "Have you made a pot before?"

"Yes, I made several pots when I was living with Maria's Lakota tribe. Spending some of my winter in the

West was better than waiting for the growing season to come again here on the farm. I really enjoyed it." Sam got his hands into the clay bowl and began mixing and forming it. "It's very relaxing."

Sarah began, "Sam had a piece of Masonite board that could cover the kitchen table. With two of you on this side, one on the other, and Sam and I at the two ends, we can all have fun making pots and still protect the table surface. The pots have to be fired after we've formed them. But that takes about twenty-four hours, and we have no kiln. Sam will build a bond fire in the backyard and fire them the primitive, old-fashioned way."

"We also don't have any potting wheels," Sam explained as he walked around the table, giving each an equal portion of clay. "So, we'll use the coil method."

Tucker was silent. He just wanted to learn. His need to talk was over-powered by his fascination with actually making a Native American pot.

Sam went on. "This technique involves rolling clay into long ropes." He demonstrated forming a long, snake-like cord, like a child playing with Klean Klay. "Next, stack and join the coils to build the walls of a pot." He wrapped the long clay ropes around and around. "Then we smooth the coils together. This method is a common form of hand-building, as it can be done without a potter's wheel."

Sam demonstrated as Sarah, Tucker, and his friends watched. Then, Sam took a small amount of clay, flattened it, and shaped it into a plate-shaped circle. With a plum-size piece of clay, he began rolling and shaping a piece of the blob into a rope on the smooth surface of the Masonite. "I'm making a coffee cup," he said as he kept rolling the rope between his hands. When the long piece was about the size of Betsy's third grade jumping rope, he formed it on the base and wound it around. "Okay, you all begin like I did. I'll just continue to stack the coils on top of each other until they reach the height I'd like for a big cup of coffee. Then I'll make a sturdy handle."

"I don't drink coffee," Tucker talked to himself. "But a big cup of cocoa would be great."

Sam stood back and studied his cup. "When you think it's the right size, you score each coil and join it to the one below it with slip."

Tucker looked up from rope making. "Slip? What's that?"

Sam kept his eyes on the cup he was creating. "Slip is a clay and water mixture. You smooth it all over and blend the rope pieces together." He stopped to add, "The last step is to finish the surface on the inside and the outside by smoothing the entire pot to create a seamless finish. Some potters like to leave it so you can see some of the coils. I like to have a finished, smooth pot, or cup in this case."

Tucker dipped his fingers in the little cup of slip Sam had passed around. "Coils would be too hard to keep clean." Tucker thought of the pitcher pump that Gramma still had in the kitchen sink. She'd pump the handle until the teapot was full, then put the kettle on the stove to bring to a boil. That was just step one in washing dishes. Nope, his cup would be smooth. He could rinse the cup quickly after he drank the last bit of cocoa. He'd have a special spot to store it in the cabinet. It was his cup, and only his germs would be on it. He would make it as simple as possible. He looked at the pots the others were making. Wow, they were all great. Christy was making a bowl. Freddie's would have to wait until it was finished. He had no idea what he was making. But it didn't matter. It was fun! "What a great vacation."

Chapter Eight
SING A STORY OF THE OLD WEST

Gramma fixed a big casserole of macaroni and cheese for dinner. "You've been all over, Tucker. I imagine you're hungry. Carolyn and Betsy aren't here this evening. Carolyn is with Caleb at his parents' house. His mother is going to teach her how to make angel food cake in a special way. Betsy is over at Valerie's house. She called and said she'd miss supper because of something about an unfinished game of Monopoly. So, with them gone, enjoy as much macaroni and cheese as you want."

"Thanks, Gramma." He sat down at the table and waited for Grandpop to offer grace. "I won't be home after dinner either. Christy, Freddie, and maybe Micky, are going with me to a movie."

"Oh my, Micky too." She put the large baking dish on the hot pads she had already placed on the table, waiting for the just-out-of-the-oven dish. "Now take your time eating, Tucker. You could choke if you wolf it down."

Tucker put the first bite in his mouth and savored the sharp taste of the cheddar cheese. He closed his eyes, enjoying every creamy bite. "Gramma, this is the best."

His grandmother smiled. "You always say that, Tucker."

Grandpop buttered a piece of bread from edge to edge. "What movie are you and your friends going to see?"

"*The Westward Trail*," Tucker said, trying to swallow fast. "It should be a really good one. It's a western."

"Okay," he said with a smile. "A western." Starting to eat, he added, "You and Sam Treadway are closer related than I thought. You both love the old west."

"You're not a cowboy fan, Grandpop?" Tucker was amazed. "How could anyone not love a great ride on a horse."

Uncle Jabob chuckled quietly. Putting down his fork, he said, "Tell him about it, Dad."

"Tucker," Grandpop said and laughed, "you forget. It's not new to me. I was an Eastern cowboy. There weren't cars when I was young. We rode horses, drove horses hitched to buggies and wagons, fed horses, and mucked out the barn where the horses bedded down." He scooped up another big bite of cheesy goodness. "And, yes, I love horses. I would have loved the beauty of the wide, open spaces of the west."

"I like that, Grandpop." Tucker's thoughts flitted to a man in a Stetson hat driving a buckboard across the hilly, rocky plains of the old west. It felt like the dust that had blown in, was in his throat.

Tucker finally piled the last bite of elbow macaroni and sunshine-yellow cheese on his fork, finished his meal, washed it down with sweet ice tea, and excused himself from the table. When the telephone rang, Tucker stopped and answered.

Freddie brought Tucker up to date. "Anna said her mother planned to take her to Ziesel's Department Store to get a new Easter dress this afternoon. So, she's not able to go to the movie."

Tucker scooped up his car key where he had left it on a living room side-table, his jacket from the hall tree, and darted out the door.

That meant that Tucker would drive his own car. He pulled the A Model up in front of Christy's house. She ran out to the car, buttoning her jacket as she went. Freddie and Micky started over from the Coopers' nearby home.

"I'm glad I got here first in case Freddie changes his mind about sitting in the rumble seat." She opened the door and slid onto the seat.

Tucker had pulled up the upholstered front-facing seat from where it had been folded into the rear of his car, like opening a trunk backward and pulling out a second seat, the rumble seat. "Hop in, Freddie," he called out the open window. Seeing the blanket in Freddie's arms, he added, "Looks like you and Micky are prepared to sit in the open rumble seat."

"You bet ya." Freddie laughed and helped Micky into the back.

"Ready everyone?" Tucker called out.

Micky waved his arms in the air and wore an excited smile. "Let's go."

"I am thrilled," Christy bubbled. "I love the Singing Cowboy, Eddie Dean."

"I like his horse, Copper," Tucker said with a Western accent he had developed from the many movies he had seen. Then he laughed.

Once they got to the theater, each of them got out their ticket money. Since Micky was only five, Freddie's dad had given him fifteen cents for admission. Tucker, Christy, and Freddie's ticket price was thirty-five cents each.

The theater lobby smelled like popcorn smothered in butter. There were other sweets and treats, but the smell of corn in the paper bag over-powered it all. Tucker had just eaten, but he considered that meal an appetizer. He chose the large ten cent bag, the one intended for passing and sharing. The others ordered the nickel bag. Freddie whispered out of the corner of his mouth, "I'll probably finish off Micky's bag, too."

"I heard that," Micky asserted as he held the warm popcorn close. "I can eat all of this. Why do you think I asked the lady to add extra butter all over the top?"

Freddie rolled his eyes. "I wouldn't be surprised." He handed Micky some waded up paper. "Here's a lot of napkins. With all of that butter, it sounds like you'll need them."

The theater was starting to darken when they took their seats. Micky was glad that there was a Donald Duck cartoon that came on first. Donald's nephews Huey, Dewey, and Louie were their usual mischievous characters, as the colorful characters pranced through the film. All four of them laughed through the short cartoon.

When the News reel came on, with images of the continuing cleanup of European cities following the bombings of World War II, Micky covered his eyes. There was so much debris, the cleanup crew bulldozed it into a rubble hill in the middle of town and planted grass on it.

The thrilling music of the feature movie was a welcomed relief. The story in *The Westward Trail* unfolded on the screen. A woman from the city moved west to run a ranch with her brother. Tucker wondered if a city girl would be able to tame the West. However, a greedy saloon owner wanted their ranch land. With hard work, digging, and drilling, a silver mine was found on the land. After the murder of the sheriff, the singing lawman organized the other ranchers to fight back. It was perfect. Music and singing for Christy, and strong cowboys for the guys.

Tucker, after having lived with his elderly grandparents all of his life, was absorbed in a time gone by. His grandfather was three-years-old when Abraham Lincoln was killed. Tucker was a 1948 era boy with an 1865 view of life. The movie was a special visit "home."

All the way back to Dunlap, Tucker kept repeating, "I didn't have to work at Butch's station, we went to a great movie, and, there was no school or homework. This is the most relaxing, fun, playful holiday I've ever had."

Chapter Nine
SOWING THE SEED

When Tucker got home from the movie late in the afternoon, the family settled into a rhythm that was repeated most Saturdays. To some it may have been boring. To Tucker, the sameness felt safe.

Uncle Jacob closed the March 15th issue of *Life* magazine with the cover of actor Laurence Olivier as Hamlet. "There was a great article on our government facing the realities of the Communists. But, I need a break from another discussion of a campus riot at LSU."

It was a lot to read about childish college students in one evening. Uncle Jacob rubbed his eyes and stretched. "Tucker, will you come outside and help me."

"Sure." Tucker put his baseball glove down. "I'll finish oiling my glove later." Baseball practice had just started the week before, and they were now on vacation. There would be plenty of time to prepare his gear over Easter break.

Uncle Jacob buttoned his sweater. "I'm going to sow a little grass seed over near the garden. We're wearing a path where we all walk in through the garden gate from the alley." He reached for the doorknob with Joe on his heals. "I'll toss the seed, and you watch to see if I miss any spots." Uncle Jacob walked down off the side porch just as Tucker finished putting away the glove oil on the hall closet shelf.

"No, Tiny, stay," Tucker ordered the little dog. "Gramma wants you to be in here with her." Tucker went outside and smiled as he rounded the corner of the house and saw the tepee standing tall in the small orchard. "At least I did something right," he mumbled to himself. "Wow," he whispered.

Joe's dense and wiry dog hair was shedding it's outer, winter coat and left strands on Tucker's pants when he brushed against his boy. Joe kept walking slowly over to the tepee. He didn't go in. Laying on the ground at the opening, he appeared to be on guard as he had during the war.

"But, Uncle Jacob," Tucker said as he caught up, "they said on the radio that tomorrow's weather was going to be windy. Won't the seed be blown all over the yard?"

Uncle Jacob kept walking in his quiet manner. "I think most of it will stay on the ground." He rubbed the toe of his shoe in the patchy grass near the side gate. "I thought if I seed this small patch, and then you get the bucket over there by the shed and water the seeded area real good, that should hold the Kentucky Bluegrass in place."

"I just thought, if it's windy tomorrow," Tucker kept talking and walking to the outside yard pump, "that's going to make batting practice hard on Monday, if it's still blowing."

Uncle Jacob pulled a large burlap sack of grass seed from behind the lawnmower in the storage shed. Like the man in a famous painting by Vincent van Gogh, called, *The Sower*.[5] Uncle Jacob reached into the bag, grabbed a handful of seed, and tossed it onto the small patch at his feet. "It doesn't seem like the coach would call a practice during the vacation."

Tucker put the old wooden bucket under the spout of the pitcher pump that stood several yards from the summer kitchen door and raised the pump handle. "Coach said he's going to show up if batters want to come and practice. He said it's not mandatory." He pumped several times as water flowed from the spout into the bucket.

"That sounds fair," Uncle Jacob agreed as he continued to toss the seed.

Tucker carried the bucket over to the area of sparse grass and set it on the ground. With the ladle that hung from the Myers pump, he waved the mega spoon over the seed and sprinkled it like the clouds had opened for a light rain.

"That should do it," Uncle Jacob said as he threw his last handful. "I picked up a couple of Almond Joy candy bars for you. I know you like the chewy coconut inside. Eat them both now, or save one. Dinner won't be for a few hours."

Back in the house, Uncle Jacob poured another cup of coffee and settled down to continue reading the rest of that week's *Life* magazine. Slouching on the couch,

Tucker pealed back the wrapper of his first candy bar and bit off a large chunk. Then, he jumped up, gathered a half dozen comic books, and went out onto the front porch to enjoy the late day sun.

The sky was the bluest he had seen in the previous month of overcast skies, rain, and sleet. He eyed the porch swing, the perfect place to enjoy the day. Stretching out on the wooden swing, he put Gramma's soft back cushion under his head.

The service bell at Butch Randolf's Sinclair station across the street, announced another customer, as drivers filled up their gas tanks for the weekend. Since Butch had no brakes to fix or oil to change that afternoon, he didn't need Tucker to work the drive and pump the gas. Tucker had the Saturday off, and it couldn't have been a better day to enjoy it.

Chapter Ten
A DRIVE AND A MOTOR

Late in the afternoon, after the tepee was in place, the seed had been sown, both candy bars had been eaten, and dinner wasn't on the table yet, Tucker jumped into his Model A and drove around the neighborhood. He wanted to fill up on sunshine on one of the prettiest days in quite a while. The sun shone overhead, and a breeze was touching everything with sweetness. It was glorious.

To be honest, it was more than that. Tucker was a doer. It was impossible for him to stay in one place for very long. He would find something to do rather than loosing brain power just sitting and doing nothing.

He enjoyed the gentle hum of the car around him, and the light shining through the windshield. At the next corner, he turned right on Harvest Avenue, and drove toward Aunt Cora and Uncle Jerry's house on the next corner.

There was a sameness about his neighborhood that was comforting. Uncle Jerry worked at Miles Laboratory, but he was always inventing little things. Some of the family didn't understand his ability to see a need before it occurred. But Tucker did and usually listened to his newest thoughts.

Tucker turned right in front of Aunt Cora's house, then maneuvered around until he came out on a road that was a combination of rural and suburban. Driving along the Mishawaka Road, where farmland mixed with newly built, post-war houses, Tucker soon came upon Avril Mosher's century old farm.

The red barn out back, with its stone foundation and bank entrance, looked like a painting Tucker had seen in the Art room at school. He wondered if the teacher had painted it using Mosher's barn as his "model."

He saw Mr. Mosher dragging a small barrel from his barn out to the road. The container was packed to the brim and wobbled when he rolled over the pebbles at the side of the road. Suddenly, one of the pieces of whatever Avril had on top of his barrel slipped off and fell on the side of the road. To Tucker, it looked like a small motor.

He slowed the car and pulled into Mosher's long and winding driveway. "What ya doin'?"

"Hi, Tucker," Avril said with an exhausted, grumpy sound. Everyone for miles around knew Tucker McBride.

Mr. Mosher's glasses drooped down his nose, and he kept pushing them up. "My repair shop in the corner of the barn is so full, I'm tripping over stuff. I have to get rid of a bunch of junk that doesn't work, and I don't have time to fix it anymore." He stooped down and picked the small motor off the ground. "Sometimes, I wish the tooth fairy would take all of this junk away."

Tucker raised his eyebrows. "I don't think that's the tooth fairy's job."

"Maybe not. But a fella can wish." Mr. Mosher positioned the barrel in the grass at the side of the road. "I don't want anyone to hit it. The stuff has no value, but their car does."

Mr. Mosher seemed overwhelmed to Tucker. He had never seen the man that way. He couldn't believe it. Avril Mosher was a man of many talents. Tucker tried to stay calm and muffled a measure of concern behind his ball cap. "Are you okay, Mr. Mosher?"

"Oh, don't mind me. I'm just tired and want to get this stuff out of the barn. WOWO's radio program, *Down on the Farm*, announced that we could have some bad weather. I want this done."

"If you don't want that motor you just plopped back on top of your pile, I'll help you out by taking it off your hands." Tucker held his breath and waited for an answer.

Avril stretched his back and moaned. "That motor had been on my son's bicycle. It's missing parts, and he's over twenty-one and drives a Ford truck. I'm done with that one. It's yours." The corners of his mustache finally turned up.

If Tucker had some fuzz under his lip, he would have curled his mustache. "That is super, Mr. Mosher. Thank you."

"No. I need to thank you, Tucker. If you want to come by tomorrow and go through all of this junk, feel free." Mr. Mosher puffed out his chest. "It feels good, with you taking just one piece of this stuff off my hands."

"If I can find room for it in Grandpop's shed, I'll take some more stuff. I like to tinker." He took the motor and smiled. It would make a fun evening or Sunday afternoon pastime project.

Chapter Eleven
UP ALONE

That evening, Grandpop went to bed at 8 p.m. as usual. After a lifetime of working on the railroad and getting up while others were still sleeping, the habits of sleep had been permanently stored in his body.

Gramma had brought her old, dark brown sewing basket into the living room and sat in her small rocker. Turning a sock inside out, she pulled the darning egg from the basket and inserted it into the stocking. Stretching the sock over the egg, she began closing the many holes in Betsy's socks. With a double thread, she created parallel threads vertically, then wove a second set of threads horizontally, to cover the hole.

Gramma wasn't ready for bed. At eight o'clock, the musical program she had been waiting to hear began to sing out on the radio. Her many stitches seemed to follow the rhythm of the music. She stopped stitching, closed her eyes, and smiled as a gifted soprano hit some high notes.

Tucker sat on the floor with some old newspapers spread out in front of him to protect that area of the carpet from any oil that might fall from his new project. He sat cross legged, a custom that was becoming very comfortable. He had the little motor in front of him and a few small tools in each hand.

At nine o'clock, the *Aldrich Family* would come on with the same opening words, "Hen-ry-y-y-y! Hen-ry Aldrich!" Then Henry's response, in a cracking teenage voice, "Com-ing Mother!" Gramma and Tucker both liked the radio show, if she could stay awake until it was over.

Uncle Jacob was a fast reader with an outstanding memory. Henry Aldrich was finished with his current escapade, at the same time Jacob finished the book. "Maw, are you still awake?"

Gramma put her darning back in the basket, looked around, and checked the wall clock. "I think Henry Aldrich and I will end the day together. Tucker, are you staying up?"

Tucker didn't look up from his new fun project. He didn't know what program would come on next, but he could easily listen and tinker at the same time. "I'm getting an idea of how to fix this motor. I'll go to bed soon."

Uncle Jacob went into the entry hall and wiggled the door handle. "I'll lock this door but not the side one. Your sisters aren't home yet. After Betsy and Carolyn come in, you can turn off the lights and lock up. I checked the door in the summer kitchen a few hours ago when I filled my coffee cup."

"Okay, good night," Tucker said without taking his eyes off the nuts and bolts in front of him. He heard

Uncle Jacob hit the upper landing just as the next radio program came on. Tucker stopped.

"Suspense Theater," the speaker's deep, sinister voice announced. Tucker's blood ran cold. He shuddered as the announcer began with eerie music under the words:

"And so, to conspire with you, the radio Columbia Broadcasting System presents *Suspense*, a series of tales well calculated to keep you ... in *suspense*."

Tucker immediately rethought his evening. Maybe he didn't want to stay up longer after all. As he began to anxiously shove the motor parts and pieces into a cardboard box, the back door rattled. Catching his breath in his throat and closing his eyes tightly, he turned toward the sound.

"Hi, Tucker," Betsy announced as she breezed in. "You're still up?"

"Just going to bed," he said stiffly, pretending to be brave. He placed the box of motor parts on the dining room table. "How was the movie?"

"It was great," she announced, hanging her jacket on the hall tree in the front hall. She bounced over to the box of motor parts, with the wholesome energy she got from the family-friendly movie.

"What did you and your friends see?" Tucker wanted to turn the light out and dash up the stairs. But Carolyn wasn't in yet.

"The movie? *I Remember Mama*," Betsy answered as she headed for the stairs. "It was about the everyday life of a family and stared Irene Dunne. It kinda reminded me of our house." Yawing, she added, "It was fantastic. I'm going up to bed."

With his sister upstairs, the voices on the radio crept into his awareness again. He had to lock up and turn off the scary radio. Just as he started to reach for the lock, the door popped open. Tucker nearly jumped out of his shoes.

"Tucker." Carolyn started as she breezed in and hung up her coat. "Tomorrow is Sunday. You'd better go to bed." Being the oldest sister, Carolyn often felt like she needed to watch over her youngest brother.

He locked the door with a snap of the skeleton key. There was always a non-step in locking the door that he couldn't forget. Rather than hanging the key on a hook, he had to remember to leave the key in the lock. With the key in the lock, someone couldn't open the door by putting another skeleton key in the hole. Quickly, he turned off the dining room light and the scary radio program. "Did you and Caleb get some of the painting done at your future house?"

"Two rooms," she answered quickly and started up the steps. Then she turned. "We're not married yet, but it's still my house. I have beige in the living and dining rooms, and white in the kitchen. I always wanted a white house."

"Yep," Tucker agreed, then finally turned off the radio and lights and followed on Carolyn's heals. She would be the last one in, since their brother, Tim, was in the Marines.

Upstairs, Tucker got ready for bed. He pulled an old sweatshirt over his head. It wasn't fit for school anymore. He had worn it to play touch football in the field down by the creek and had rolled into a wild blueberry patch. Looking in the mirror, Tucker convinced himself that his need to go to bed on time, even during school break, was due to the next day being Palm Sunday, not because the radio program had shivered his spine. Feeling a little guilty about being a coward, he convinced himself he had to get to church on time to support Gus as he read the scripture for the morning. After all, Tucker had volunteered Gus's participation in the service. The least he could do was arrive before his cousin started playing the prelude.

Chapter Twelve
PALM SUNDAY

The congregation stood as Paulene Gisselman led the choir procession up the center isle of the church in their maroon robes with white stoles hanging down the front. Everyone sang the Palm Sunday hymn, "Hosanna, Loud Hosanna."[6] For the most part, it was inspiring.

Gladis Graber's pitch was a little off that morning, but she seemed to slide into the proper note eventually. Her ability to find the pitch among all the voices around her, probably was due to cousin Sharon increasing the volume as she played the organ, so the music could sound sweeter.

Tucker especially liked the part when Homer Zigbee brought up the end of the procession with his rich, deep voice that seemed to rumble in Tucker's bones. There were several other basses, but no one could sing those low notes like Homer. Even from the first row of the balcony, where Tucker and his friends stood, he could feel the vibration of the bass voices, like the oom-pah of a band.

To Tucker, there was something about music in church that brought out the meaning of worship. His love of the hymns may have been from sitting beside Grandpop when he was young. At that time, Gramma played the pump organ every Sunday, while Grandpop shepherded Tucker. Sitting beside him, he could feel his grandfather's deep voice vibrate the wood in the pew they leaned against. That seemed to plant the glory of God down deep inside where it became his "bone knowledge." Tucker sang out without looking at the hymnal. *Hosanna, Loud Hosanna, the little children sang.* [5] Mr. Zigbee's voice bellowed out an oom pah, oom pah pah pah.

It was a glorious start to the morning. The sun streamed through the stain glass windows behind the chancel. The window had been dedicated to Tucker's great-grandparents and bore their names.

Christy and Freddie were on each side of him. Anna Frederic sat on the other side of Freddie, a usual position for Miss Woe, as Anna Frederick had been called since she graduated from elementary school. Yvonne Sherbet was next to Anna which only emphasized Yvonne being about six inches shorter. Gilbert, Raymond, Ralph, and Darla sat in the row behind them. From there, they could whisper over the shoulders in front of them and be a part of the group, rather than a fringe participant.

Their Sunday school teacher, Birdie Kline, sat nearby each week. Tucker was always aware of her presence and assumed she was there to hover over them, making sure their whispers didn't get too loud.

In the pulpit, Pastor Daily stood through the hymn and prepared to lead the congregation in the Call to Worship and Opening Prayer. "From Matthew 21:1-4," he began. "Please follow where it is printed in your bulletin."

Leader: "And when they drew nigh unto Jerusalem, and were come to Bethphage, unto the mount of Olives, then sent Jesus two disciples, Saying unto them, 'Go into the village over against you, and straightway ye shall find an ass tied, and a colt with her: loose *them*, and bring *them* unto me.'"

People: "Lord, may I, like the disciples, obey when Jesus calls me to action."

Leader: "And if any *man* say ought unto you, ye shall say, 'The Lord hath need of them'; and straightway he will send them."

People: "Today, I choose to not be afraid, and to speak out in the name of Jesus."

Across the large pulpit, Pastor Daily folded his hands in prayer. "Let us pray. Oh Lord God, creator of all that was created, Holy is your name. On this day in which we remember your son, Jesus's triumphant entry into Jerusalem on the back of a donkey, we ask that we, like Jesus, follow your call, regardless of how magnificent or humble it may seem. The love and offering are the same. In the name of Jesus, we pray. Amen."

Tucker thought the morning prayer was different. It was so much shorter than the pastor usually prayed. Somehow, it seemed more profound, more urgent. And, Tucker wondered, why?

"Please sit down," Pastor Daily continued. "Now, we have a special treat this morning. Young Micky, the Coopers' nephew and house guest, is going to sing a song his mother composed for him, *Good Morning Jesus*[7], and our organist will accompany him."

"What?" Freddie whispered in a not so soft voice. Leaning over to Tucker, he added, "No one told me."

Tucker nodded and covered his mouth. "I don't think even Gramma knew. Even though she doesn't play the organ anymore, she does add to the music at the piano. She knows all the musical plans for morning worship."

Christy leaned over from Tucker's other side. "Maybe she knew he was going to sing and helped to keep Micky's secret. He's a cute kid."

Birdie Kline cleared her throat.

Micky stepped aside as a stool was placed at the foot of the lectern. In his navy-blue suit, white shirt, and bright yellow necktie with the face of a collie dog in the lower middle, he stepped up boldly like he had done it many times.

Sputters and whispers of joy and encouragement filled the sanctuary. "Isn't he cute?" and, "What a big boy."

Tucker was amazed. Micky's poise in front of the congregation looked like a high schooler who had shrunk down to fit the outfit he was wearing. When the organ started playing the introduction, Tucker leaned forward with his hands on his knees.

Good morn-ing, Je-sus. Good morn-ing, Je-sus.

Let me sit on your lap and start my day.

Hal-le-lu-jah, praise your name. I am one of your lambs.

Good noon to Je-sus. Good noon to Je-sus.

Help me find a new friend, to bring your way.

Hal-le-lu-jah, praise your name. I am one of your lambs.

Good even-ing, Je-sus. Good even-ing, Je-sus.

I had a spe-cial day with you to-day.

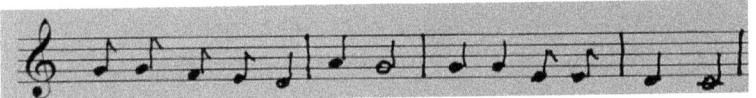

Hal-le - lu-jah, praise your name. I am one of your lambs.

While it wasn't the custom of the church to clap during the service, Micky's song was too precious to go unanswered. As the congregation applauded, Micky put his hand across his waist, bowed, and then joined his aunt and uncle, Freddie's parents, in the third row.

Pastor Daily was still clapping when he returned to the pulpit. "Thank you, Micky." As the boy settled in the pew, the pastor took out a pen and poised it over the back of the bulletin. "Are there any prayer requests this morning? I know some of our military men still need our prayers. The war is over. But the daily war of dealing with injury and anxiety still remains with many."

Roger Wilmington's wife, June, asked for prayer for Roger. "I know he won't say anything, but he hurt his hand yesterday. He was hanging a picture for me and hit his left hand that was holding the nail. Prayers would be appreciated."

Abagail Lemming needed prayers for her mother. Mrs. Lemming was not an outgoing or bold woman. Her voice was as soft and timid as her manner. Tucker had to strain to hear what she said. There was something about a downed tree and tripping. But, he couldn't hear what happened to her mother.

Pastor Daily then bowed in prayer for those whose names had been lifted up. Tucker smiled. Though Daily was young, he always sounded a little like Tucker's grandfather when he prayed.

Next on the morning bulletin was the scripture reading. Tucker held his breath as Gus stepped up to the lectern. Would he stumble and trip? Would his voice crack, or would he be barely heard? Tucker felt a little guilty in the pit of his stomach. He was the one who had volunteered Gus to read the scripture. Or, maybe the queasy feeling was because he was hungry already. He wasn't sure which was true. But then, he was always hungry. Tucker watched intently. Gus seemed to stand tall and straight. His face was relaxed, and he even smiled at his mother.

Gus turned the pages of the large pulpit Bible and began. "John 12:12 through 19. On the next day much people that were come to the feast, when they heard that Jesus was coming to Jerusalem, took branches of palm trees, and went forth to meet him, and cried, Hosanna: Blessed is the King of Israel that cometh in the name of the Lord.

"And Jesus, when he had found a young ass, sat thereon; as it is written,

"Fear not, daughter of Sion: behold, thy King cometh, sitting on an ass's colt.

"These things understood not his disciples at the first: but when Jesus was glorified, then remembered they that these things were written of him, and that they had done these things unto him.

"The people therefore that was with him when he called Lazarus out of his grave, and raised him from the dead, bare record.

"For this cause the people also met him, for that they heard that he had done this miracle.

"The Pharisees therefore said among themselves, Perceive ye how ye prevail nothing? behold, the world is gone after him."[8]

Closing the Bible, he walked slowly and confidently down the few steps to sit with his parents, George and Nancy Guston, in the first row. Nancy removed her spring-white gloves and patted Gus's cheek. Tucker wondered what the touch of a mother would feel like.

Chapter Thirteen
THE CLASS

Sunday school always followed the church service. No one in Tucker's class thought of skipping. It was a chance to see all their friends again. But it was also an opportunity to sample a new kind of cookie their teacher, Mrs. Kline, found in an old cookbook or one of her *Better Homes and Gardens* magazines. She kept at least the last six months issues on the over-loaded coffee table in her living room. It never occurred to her to throw any of them away.

"Class," Birdie began as she plopped a basket, decorated with a colorful gold bow, on the table. "The cookie of the day is chocolate and peppermint chip."

"Oh, my goodness," Darla gasped. "That sounds like a double blast of goodness."

Mrs. Kline sighed, like an over-dramatic actress. "Oh, my dear, it is. They are marvelous. I made a double batch. My Harvey ate three of them last evening."

"I'll pass them out for you," Christy offered as the room began to fill with a rich chocolate and peppermint smell.

Mrs. Kline looked quickly at Tucker. "Thanks, but, only one each. If anyone wants a second, that will cost ten cents for our Easter basket food ministry."

"But," Freddie stammered, "I didn't bring any money with me."

"That's alright. I'll take an I.O.U." She paused before handing over the cookies to one of Tucker-the-cookie-eater's best friends. "But, you have to earn the money to pay off the I.O.U. Your mother can't just give it to you. You'll have to do something special for it. I don't mean your normal regular chores. Like wash the windows or clean out the refrigerator."

Christy held the basket by the handle. "I feel a little like Little Red Riding Hood." Approaching Tucker, she offered, "My, what big teeth you have. They are the better to eat a cookie with, my friend."

After Christy circled the room slowly, Mrs. Kline opened the lesson with, "Now that you have a mouth full, I'll begin today's lesson."

Gilbert laughed, spraying cookie crumbs around the room. "Sorry," Gilbert sputtered as more crumbs flew.

Mrs. Kline pointed to a stack of Scott paper napkins. "There's some napkins in the basket." She watched Gilbert wipe his mouth.

Tucker smiled. It was obvious, Gilbert wouldn't slow down Mrs. Kline's lesson. She had taught the junior high class for years. This particular group may have been more of a challenge, but they were all bright and loving.

"Before you begin," Tucker reached into the cookie basket, "I want two more cookies. These are great. Here's a quarter. Keep the change."

"Well, thank you, Tucker." Mrs. Kline put the coin in a small cup she had placed in the basket. "Anyone else?"

Christy, Freddie, and Yvonne selected a second cookie. Anna said she was watching her sugar level and would pass on a second one. A few of the others selected a second cookie, too.

"I owe you," Freddie offered as he bit into the cookie. He place a small piece of paper with "I.O.U." written on it and his name.

Mrs. Kline flipped the cover over the back of the felt board she had prepared. "Everyone in Jerusalem came out to celebrate Jesus's entry into town on Palm Sunday. They believed that he was the long-awaited Messiah who would save them from Roman rule." She placed a green felt palm branch on the board. "He didn't come into town on the back of a mighty war horse. He rode in on a humble donkey, but the people saw a warrior. Now, when we see pictures of Jesus on the small animal, we see the lamb of God who saves us from sin."

She placed a fabric cutout of a small white lamb, innocent and beautiful. "See the lamb's eyes, he's waiting for you."

Tucker had never thought of Palm Sunday like that before. It was always centered around the palm fronds the pastor sent home with every family. Gramma draped them around the wall clock where they remained for months. She only took them down when all of the blades turned brown and started falling on the floor.

Mrs. Kline continued. "Like our hymn reminded us this morning, the children sang, 'Hosanna.' In Hebrew it means, 'Save us. Please, help us.' Now we think of Hosanna as a word of praise. And, it wasn't just children who shouted and danced as he came into town. It was the adults, too. They spread palm branches in his path like they would if he were a king. And, remember, Palm Sunday was before, before everything that happened." She put a felt crown on the board.

The class listened intently, silently, an unusual happenstance for that class. "Everyone," she offered softly, "there's always a day or time before, before everything. On Palm Sunday, no one knew that something else was coming, or that God would take that something and make it His blessing for everyone. At the time of 'the before,' we don't know God's plan." She placed a cross on the board. "So, always remember, no matter what the day brings, God has a plan to turn it into a marvelous thing. Wonderful days can come before heart-breaking days. And heart-breaking days can turn into heart-filling days." Mrs. Kline put up a cut out piece that represented an open cave with a stone rolled away. "God is always there with us and has a plan for something better. We just don't know it at the time. I ask you to believe it. Because believing helps us to endure the hard days."

"Mrs. Kline," Anna interrupted, "what if you don't like the bad days?"

"You're not expected to like the bad days. You are expected to ask God to walk with you through those difficult times, and He will."

"Woe, is me," Anna said with a smile. "Just one more 'woe,' then I'm done."

Mrs. Kline explained. "Anna, it's a little like taking a walk in the woods on a beautiful autumn day. The path is a clear, winding stretch of dirt and gravel. The trees are magnificent, red, gold, and fall-green. You are enjoying that day, the day before, and don't think about what would follow. That's the day 'before,' the heart-filling day. Then the wind blows fierce through the boughs and branches. Every glorious leaf falls from the trees and are trampled into dust, or blown far away. That's a heart-breaking day for those who love the color of autumn and do not know what happens next. But, when you ask God to walk with you through the bitter cold of winter, when all color turns to white, then to the gunk of mud, you are filled with the sparkling crystals of hope. Next, is the heart-filling days, when God fulfills His promise and green leaves bud out. For every bad day, there is a different, beautiful day."

"Wow," Anna whispered. "Not woe."

"Well, woe or wow, class, I want you to read Chapters 21-28 of Matthew as you prepare for Holy Week. That is the 'after,' between the 'before,' and then the 'heart-filling miracle.' Start reading the passage today, and read it again every day, until we meet again on Easter Sunday."

Chapter Fourteen
A FAMILY GATHERING

Tucker rushed home after Sunday school. When he walked into the house, the crispy gold of frying chicken perfumed the air. In the kitchen, he found Aunt Cora slipping the pieces of fried chicken she had breaded and fried before church, into the oven to warm. Tucker didn't miss the cake carrier she also brought in and sat on the table.

Cora lifted the lid of the carrier and beamed with satisfaction. "See, Mother, it's the pineapple upside down cake recipe Sam Treadway's mother always baked. It has a cherry in each hole created by the center of every pineapple."

"Ja, gut, Cora. It looks wunderbar." Opening the utensil drawer, Gramma pulled out a sharp paring knife. "I have all these potatoes to peel, Cora. I could use your help. Would you peel a few?"

"How did you keep the cake away from Uncle Jerry?" Tucker laughed and took off his casual jacket and hung it on one of the pegs beside the door. "I'll peel the potatoes for you."

"Hello, the house," Gramma's cousin Sam called as he and his wife, Sarah, popped in through the side door. "We came to see the tepee."

"Tepee?" Uncle Jerry and Luke sputtered at the same time. "A Native American tepee?"

"Sure," Tucker said with his usual smile. "Christy, Freddie, Micky, and I set it up Friday after school."

"Go, go," Gramma said with a laugh. "Cora can peel the potatoes for me. When you all finish inspecting the Indian dwelling, get back in here. Sam, I'm glad you and Sarah are staying for lunch. There's plenty of chicken. Joseph plucked feathers from two nice hens last evening. James and Franny will be here with their four children soon. Since David's service is just getting over and he's hanging up his clerical robe, he, Karen, and their two will get here in about a half hour. Karen is bringing a big pot of green beans[14]. She always cooks them perfectly."

"I have two cherry pies." Sarah joined in dinner preparations. "Where do you want me to put them, Rebecca?"

Gramma started pealing potatoes. "You can put the pies on the sideboard. That would be fine."

Tucker grabbed his coat again and motioned for his cousin Luke, Uncle Jerry, and Sam to follow him. Sarah would not be left out and joined the hunt for a tepee.

When they got to the orchard, Luke stopped. "The natives have set up camp," he whispered in caution.

"Not the natives," Sam said with a chuckle. "Tucker put my tepee together Friday afternoon."

"Not just Tucker," Christy corrected as she walked into the yard and joined the group.

"Me too," Micky demanded with his chin jutted out. "I was here. I helped."

"Micky wasn't the only Cooper," Freddie boasted. "We all put it together."

"Well, you all did a great job." Sam patted Tucker and Micky on their backs. "I couldn't have done a better job." He walked around to the side, then added, "There's just one thing. The Lakota, part of the Great Sioux Nation, modified their tepees. They tilted the entire cone-shaped structure into the wind. That makes the tepee look a little less like a glamorous structure on a movie set. With it slanted, it made it almost straight in the back. The tepee could stand strong against the windy weather and gave it more space inside."

"Wow." Tucker put his hands on his hips and studied the perfectly round tepee. It looked just like an ice cream cone. "I wouldn't have noticed that. Tepees in the movies are always symmetric all the way around."

Sam laughed as he bent and entered the tepee. "The western movies made them pretty, not correct."

"I saw a western yesterday. It was great!" Micky announced as he walked to the side of the tepee and checked its shape. "I can sure see it's round. So, Mr. Treadway," he thought through what Sam had said, "the tepee should lean a little, to protect it from the wind?"

"You sure are smart," Tucker marveled. "If you want to come back after lunch, you can help me position it on a tilt. That will make it correct." Tucker knew

Micky would be there. The boy reminded him of himself when he was five.

Mr. Justine pulled into the alley with Jinx and Jason as Tucker patted Micky on the back. "Tucker, my goodness, this is amazing."

"Wow, wow, wowzer, wow!" Jinx Justine shouted out the window. "Can we go in it?"

"It's really keen!" Jason Justine called out.

"Sure," Tucker agreed. "I'll show you the inside."

The boys jumped out of the car with their dad on their heels.

Jinx got there first and paused just outside the opening. "Are you sure it's okay?"

"It's okay, Jinx. I built it, and there's no one in there." Tucker stepped aside so Mr. Justine could get in.

"Tucker," Betsy called from the house just as Uncle David and Aunt Karen pulled into the driveway. "We'll eat in about twenty minutes."

"Okay," Tucker hollered back.

"Lunch," Christy said with a snap of her fingers. "I'd better get home. See you later."

"Bye, Christy," called after her as she ran out of the orchard.

Uncle David looked over at the orchard and raised his eyebrows when he saw the structure. He asked, "What do you have here? This is fantastic."

Uncle David was just a little older than Tucker's mother. They were close when they were young and growing up. David often referred to his sister as his twin. Tucker always enjoyed when Uncle David stopped by the house. He and Gramma would stand out in the kitchen, talking about the church and politics.

"It's my tepee," Sam said stepping in. "Tucker and his friends put it up. Didn't they do a fantastic job?"

"They sure did," David said as he walked around, pointing out parts of the structure to his two young ones.

"This is the best treat ever." Jinx marveled as he came out of the tepee.

"Tucker," Betsy announced again as she came around the side of the house. "Hey, everybody ... we're almost ready to eat."

"We had better go," Mr. Justine announced and called for his boys to get into the car.

"I'll have it up all week," Tucker said as he edged backward toward the house. "If the boys want to come back, I'll be here."

"Thanks, Tucker," Jason called out the window as they pulled out of the alley.

"Food! That sounds good to me." Tucker waved his arms for the others to follow him into the house. "Freddie, Micky, I'll see you after lunch. We'll fix the tepee." He turned toward the house and food. "Uncle David?" he asked as his uncle caught up to him. "Did Aunt Karen make her great orange Jell-O salad[13]?"

David laughed and slapped him playfully on the back. "You know she did."

In the dining room, everyone gathered around the table and waited for Grandpop to offer grace. It was the same blessing, word for word, that he had prayed at every lunch and dinner for all the years Tucker could remember, and every year before. He felt warm and safe. Grandpop was a man of honor and belief.

There was fried chicken, mashed potatoes and gravy, Aunt Karen's green beans with large chunks of ham for added flavor, Aunt Franny's tall, yeasty smelling dinner rolls with a fresh pound of butter on the side for spreading, Aunt Karen's Jell-O salad, and a different pie from each family: cherry, apple, peach, and pecan.

Tucker smiled as everyone took one of Gramma's pale, cream-colored china plates with a delicate pink floral trim around the edge and began heaping it with food, family food ... and Tucker was able to be there. He didn't have to miss it or leave early to relieve Butch from his responsibilities at the station so he could get home to his family. Tucker added another crispy, golden brown fried chicken leg and a huge scoop of potatoes smothered in creamy, rich chicken gravy. His Easter vacation was turning out to be perfect.

Chapter Fifteen
A SLIGHT CORRECTION

After the lunch dishes were removed from the table, and the left-overs safely placed in the refrigerator, Tucker and Luke went back outside to enjoy the tepee again. Luke went inside first and found Micky sleeping on the ground.

"What do ya think?" Luke asked. "Should we wake him up?"

Tucker shrugged. "We probably should. When we adjust the tepee like Sam said, the outer covering might fall on him as we work. That would wake him up."

"Tucker?" Freddie called out as he rounded the corner of the house. "Have you seen Micky?"

Micky woke up when Freddie shouted his name. He blinked repeatedly and rubbed his eyes. "What?"

"There you are," Freddie snapped. "My mom is worried. I told her that you're okay. I said I'd go get you, and you'd be home within an hour." He reached down, took Micky's hand, and pulled him up. "Let's help Tucker, then get you home."

Tucker was glad they stayed. Once they moved a few poles, it would take several hands to balance the tepee and set the pole back into place. They repositioned the poles after Tucker determined the downwind, the direction in which the wind was blowing. With two and a half helpers, he was able tip the tepee as it should be in Lakota tradition. In no time, the tepee was authentic, and that felt good.

"Tucker, this looks great." Freddie marveled as he studied the structure. "I wonder what it would be like to be all alone out in the west with no one around for miles."

Tucker thought about that. He couldn't remember being alone. Well, there was the time he took his comic books out into a hammock he had stretched from the roof of the house to the top of a tree. That was relaxing, swaying up high. But, the solitude didn't last long. When Mrs. Stuart looked out her kitchen window and saw him swinging thirty feet off the ground, she ran out of her house. She reported the unusual reading spot to Gramma, and that was that.

Or, the time when he was in the first grade. He stopped and played in the mud puddles on the way home. Once again, the neighbor-lady three houses down reported his sloppy mess to his grandmother. Everybody in Dunlap knew what Tucker was doing, or heard the gossip about it later. Tucker was never alone.

He wondered what that would be like. He would have no one to talk to. But, he often talked to himself. No, he usually talked to himself if no one else was around. Alone? Hum.

Chapter Sixteen
SUNDAY AFTERNOON

It was late that Palm Sunday afternoon. The family had enjoyed the chatter and laughter of cleanup, as they cleared off the table and washed the dishes. Uncle David even pushed the non-electric carpet sweeper around the dining room to pick up every crumb.

Later, when evening was about to take over Dunlap and they had all gone home, Uncle Jacob got out his violin. In the corner of the living room, he started playing quiet Easter music. It was comforting and inspiring. Tucker, always on the move, went outside to make another inspection of the tepee.

Mr. Stuart from next door walked across the grass to see the displaced housing unit in Moyer's orchard. He shook his head and felt of the lacing pins in the front of the tepee. "Tucker, this is quite a set up. The Lakota were smart builders, and so are you. Adele said she enjoyed watching you, Christy, and the Cooper boy put it up from where she sat in her Adirondack chair in our backyard. She brought out a cup of coffee and made it a local, little theater event."

"Really? I didn't see her." Tucker felt like the star of an adventure movie. Then, after a minute, he realized he had been supervised-from-afar again. "Does she like the tepee, too?"

"Of course." Mr. Stuart walked into the tepee and took in the full Native American experience. "She said you had a little one over here, too. He was quite a worker."

"Micky? Yeah, he's Freddie's cousin." Tucker smiled when he thought of how much he enjoyed Micky. "The little guy was fascinated by the Lakota's practice of putting up their tepee on a slant, leaning into the breeze. It's supposed to make it stand stronger in the wind."

Mr. Stuart came out of the tepee and looked up into the orchard's tree branches. "Well, today the tepee will be put to the test. It's supposed to storm later with some pretty high winds. Looks like it's getting a little windy already."

Tucker checked the small flag that Grandpop had mounted beside the door to his workshop. It was flapping in the wind and stood straight out from the small building. "I helped Uncle Jacob sow grass seed yesterday. Hope it doesn't blow too much. Every gutter and downspout around Dunlap will have a fresh deposit of Kentucky Bluegrass."

Mr. Stuart nodded. "That just may be true." When he turned to leave, he added, "Young man, your tepee is great. Now, Adele and I are going to run into Goshen to check on her mother. She hasn't been well."

"I hope she feels better soon," Tucker called after him. He checked the sky again, and walked toward the house.

Grandpop was sitting in the living room in his leather Morris chair reading the recent issue of the *Reader's Digest*. He rested his feet on the Amish Mission-style stool Tucker had made in Mr. Justine's class and had given his grandfather at Christmas. The stool was made of red oak and brown maple, with slats down the sides, and a dark brown leather cushion on top.

Tucker knew that his grandfather's afternoon nap would soon fuzz the pages, but that was okay. That was Grandpop's usual late afternoon routine. He was a man of consistent habits and saw no need to learn new ones.

Uncle Jacob's music had been put to sleep as the radio came on. While the news droned on, Gramma sat in her sewing rocker embroidering yellow daisies on the corner of a new handkerchief she purchased from the dime store section of Winkler's Grocery. She believed in keeping her hands busy, even on a leisure Sunday afternoon.

Earlier that early evening, the sun had been shining brightly, so Gramma sat on the front porch for a little while. She was stitching French knots into her pattern, creating raised, textured dots above the daisies. She said, keeping her hands moving helped her arthritis. "Move um or glove um," she often said.

Uncle Jacob had put his violin back in its case and picked up the Sunday edition of the *Elkhart Truth* newspaper. Next, he moved on to the *South Bend Tribune*. He never seemed to tire of reading.

Tucker finished breezing through the *Tribune*'s multicolored comic section, then pulled out the motor project he had worked on. He smiled to himself. It couldn't have been a better weekend: a tepee stood in the yard, Tucker was full on all the fixings from the family dinner, and now he would do a little tinkering on the motor there on the living room floor.

"Tucker," his grandmother began, "please turn on the table lights. It is getting dark in here. Hope I'm not getting cataracts."

"If you are, I am too," Tucker joked as he pulled the chain on the floor lamp beside her chair and switched on the remaining lights on the tables in the room. "It sure is getting dark early. Maybe that storm is going to get here after all."

Gramma put her needle work in her lap and looked intently through the front window. "I don't like the look of that sky. Tucker, please run out and feed the chickens. Be sure to lock the door to the chicken coup before you come back in. I don't have a good feeling about the weather. I don't want any of the hens flapping away in the chicken yard."

"Sure, Gramma," Tucker agreed, grabbed his jacket and hurried out to the work shed. The sky was an eerie shade of yellow he had never seen before. Shuddering at the sight, he filled a bucket with chicken feed from the larger sack in the shed and hurried back out. Strangely, although he was only in the shed a minute, it seemed darker when he came out. Hurrying across the backyard, out the gate, and across the alley, he looked for the hens and small chicks. The birds were nowhere. Even the rooster was not in the chicken yard. Opening the gate to the enclosure that surrounded the coop, he stepped into the circular area where chicken hooey peppered the ground, and quickly entered the red wooden chicken coop. Inside the coop, the hens had already gathered their young by flapping their wings and sheltering the chicks under their bodies. Tucker realized that the chickens knew something was coming. He quickly shook chicken feed into each coop cup, darted out, and slid the wooden peg through the lock to latch the door.

With the sky toward Goshen now a ghastly black, Tucker put the bucket back in the shed and locked that door.

He hurried back into the house and plopped down on the living room floor beside the motor. "Done, Gramma. The hens had already gathered the chicks. It's looking bad out there."

"We interrupt this program," the radio announcer's voice broke through the game show laughter. "The weather bureau is predicting heavy wind and rain in the next hour in Elkhart County and the surrounding counties."

Tucker looked at the clock. It was a little after 4 p.m., but it was so dark. The clouds were gathering outside, turning everything a dark gray, even though sunset wouldn't fall until nearly 6 p.m. "Wow, Uncle Jacob, it might be windier than we expected."

Uncle Jacob didn't look up from the newspaper, but mumbled, "Um hum."

Grandpop sat on the edge of his chair opposite the large front window, searching the sky and coming darkness. When the lights in the house suddenly went out, he said, "Tucker, Betsy is upstairs. Better go tell her to come down here. The second floor is no place to be on a windy night. Carolyn is at the new house Caleb's building for them after their wedding. She is making decisions about drapes and carpet colors. She knows what she wants. She said the contractors had put a basement under their new house. They'll be okay if the wind gets really bad."

Tucker stood in front of the large window watching the sky with its blackening clouds and fierce wind. "I'll go up and get Betsy, then go over to Butch's station to get more flash light batteries. Don't know how long the lights will be out."

Upstairs, Betsy offered, "I'd go over to the station with you, if I didn't think you might get drenched before you got back across the street."

"You are so helpful." Tucker laughed.

When they both came back down stairs, Uncle Jacob used his finger to mark his place in his book. "Tucker, put on the rain parka I picked up at the Army Surplus store last week. You're the one running out into this weather. So, you're the one who needs it. I'll stay here with Mother and Dad."

Tucker was thrilled to be able to use the rain wear. He slipped on the green parka and ran his hands down the sides. It was made of a rubberized material and had metal clasps at the neck opening. In his usual, "Nah, I don't need it" fashion, he didn't put up the drawstring-styled hood.

It was unusual for Tucker to protect himself from the weather. But the document that came with the parka said it had been worn on D-Day during World War II. That was enough for him. He would have worn it on the hottest day in July, just because it had belonged to a war hero.

"I'll be right back," he announced, opened the door, and stepped out onto the front porch. The wooden swing that hung by chains from the porch ceiling bounced back and forth with every gust. For safety, he unhooked the swing and pushed it over against the railing. If the wind blew very hard, the old wood could have been shattered as it banged around on the porch.

Leaning into the wind, just like the tepee, Tucker ran along the sidewalk to where it stopped at the end of the yard. Watching frantic, white-knuckle drivers as they slowed for the turn, Tucker darted across US 33.

Across the street, he had to pull hard to open the office door to the service station. "That is strange," he said to Butch as he forced his way inside.

"You're just in time," Butch Randolf greeted while balancing out the cash register. "I'm thinking of closing early." He tore off the register tape, put a candy bar display under the counter, and made a quick swipe across the counter with the rag from his hip pocket.

"I'm glad you're open, Butch," Tucker said as he wiped blown dirt from the parka. "But, why on Palm Sunday?"

"My wife asked for a magazine after lunch. By the time I got here, others started stopping." Butch waved his hand in surrender. "So, I opened for a little while."

"Good, because we need some more flashlights batteries," Tucker explained as he watched how nervous Butch was. "Something wrong?"

"It's this storm coming in." As Butch spoke, the wind blew even harder, sending the oil can display, that was still outside beside the gas pumps, kiting across the drive. The heavy rain, the weather man had predicted, was going to come storming into Dunlap.

"I'll go out and bring it into the bay," Tucker offered as he grabbed the door knob without waiting for Butch's response. It had to be done, and Tucker was always the first to volunteer. "You open the bay door."

Butch hurried into the work area, pushed the button that opened the door to the side of the garage where the hydraulic lift was, and watched. The blowing rain was starting already, peppering Tucker in the face, out near the pumps. A clap of thunder made him jump, as it rumbled through the village. Tucker could feel the change of air pressure in his stomach.

The oil can display rack wobbled across the drive like it was running from the storm. Tucker darted after it and was able to get to the large metal shelving unit before the wind could slam it to the ground. Fighting against the wind, he pushed the display toward the building. Once he got it inside the bay, he didn't wait for the button. He grabbed the door and pulled the cord to shut it. "Wow, that wind is something."

Next, he quickly hurried into the office, picked out three batteries and another flashlight, and put a five-dollar bill on the counter. "You can give me the change tomorrow, or tell me how much I owe you. I'm going to hurry home. If you're leaving, you'd better be going, too."

"No," Butch said with a thoughtful tone. He pushed a key on the cash register and said with determination, "I'll stay open in case other people need something just like you did. If Tucker McBride can go out in this stuff to help his family, I can stay open."

"You be careful," Tucker warned. "I'll see you tomorrow, Butch." Tucker looked around and slipped the flashlight and batteries into a gunny sack that had been stuffed into a trash can. "It won't tear if this bag gets wet."

Gusts of wind pushed against Tucker's chest as he hurried out onto the drive. Staggering against the wind, he stopped abruptly at the side of the highway. Off in the distance, he heard a train barreling down the tracks.

A quick glance to the right, nothing was coming, except a single car several blocks away. *All's clear*, he thought. Plenty of time. Checking to the left, however, he froze. Several cars were racing in his direction, and he staggered back, out of their way. How was it possible? He could feel his heart beating in his chest.

A mile and a half down US 33, toward Goshen, Tucker saw an enormous, black, double-funnel tornado was ripping through the Midway Trailer Court. Trailer homes, cars, and everything families owned were being violently thrown into the air, sending all that families owned, into the wind. "It must have leveled the ground, and destroying everything," Tucker yelled into the nothingness around him.

Tucker ran across the highway, dodging the few cars that had gotten ahead of the tornado. He scrambled up the front steps and pulled on the door handle. The vacuum, caused by the tornado's drastic change in air pressure, held the door tightly as he pulled. Nearly falling backward when the door was free, he recovered his balance and darted in.

"The basement," he shouted. "Hurry, get into the basement."

"Why?" Betsy gasped. "What's going on?"

"Tornado, Betsy," Tucker gasped, gulping on each word. "There's a huge double headed tornado just down the street." He helped his grandmother to her feet and shouted at Betsy, "Move!"

"Come along, Dad," Uncle Jacob said as he helped Grandpop to his feet. On Jacob's way through the house, he picked up a flashlight from the cabinet under the windows.

They all hurried through the dining room toward the kitchen and the basement stairs. Tucker put his arm around his grandmother, steadying her as she moved as fast as she could. Grandpop had left his shoes beside his chair, which made walking harder. Tucker was worried about Grandpop's sock-covered feet. "Be careful, Grandpop. Without shoes, the steps might be slippery." The two dogs, Joe and Tiny, followed closely behind.

When they got to the basement door, Tucker was relieved. He would be able to get his family safely down below. But he knew, it wasn't over.

Chapter Seventeen
ANOTHER TORNADO

Betsy was the last one through the basement door. As she passed, Tucker whispered in her ear, "I'll be right back. I have to check on something."

"Tucker," Betsy ordered hoarsely, gritting her teeth. She pointed to the dark basement. "Get down there."

"I'll be right behind you ... in a few minutes." He closed the basement door and headed outside through the summer kitchen door.

The mighty force of wind made him stagger through the yard, his head lowered, leaning into the storm. He had to see if it was still standing.

Tucker held his breath all the way around the corner of the house. There was a long exhale when he saw his Model A still parked by the shed, and the tepee still standing over in the orchard. He couldn't believe it, but was glad it was all in place. He started toward the Lakota dwelling and stopped. What was that sound? There was another roaring noise coming from down the street, far beyond the alley, on the other side of the creek.

"A train?" Tucker gasped out loud. "In all of this weather? I wonder if it could get through without things flying at it. It's heavy enough to be a challenge for the wind."

Staggering down the alley a few yards, he came out on Harvest Avenue. The roaring sound hadn't stopped. What was all the noise? It was getting louder, blasting in his ears. Tucker stared to the right, toward Yellow Creek.

Above the tree line, beyond the creek, maybe a mile and a half away, another tornado was thundering in his direction. He couldn't move as heavy rain pelted him like gravel falling from the sky.

Just then, Mr. and Mrs. Radibush from the next street over came charging down the road in their woodie station wagon, their leaky exhaust pipe rumbling. Mrs. Radibush rolled down the window. "It's coming," she shouted. "Get inside."

Tucker couldn't move. It was hitting the ground just like the monstrous one in the other direction. The funnel cloud savagely jerked up what could have been Avril Mosher's barn over on the Mishawaka Road. Tucker watched in horror as the attack-cone turned Mosher's barn upside down, like a tantrum-throwing child angeringly dumping out a toy box. He could see the cows being flipped completely over, with their feet in the air, and then falling to the ground. And, the tornado kept coming.

When the treacherous cone-shaped twister got to the deeper, cooler water of the creek stream, it abruptly turned, stormed along the watery path up across the highway, then ran down the railroad tracks. A finger of the tornado peeled off from the larger, deadly mass of destruction, and started down Harvest Avenue toward Tucker. He tore back to the house and jerked open the summer house door. But, he had to see. Just as he turned to face the window in the door, the black whirring cloud roared nearer.

Within seconds, the sliver roared Tucker's way like an arrow blasting dangerously up the street toward the church. Mrs. Graber's handmade quilt bedspread that Gramma's quilting bee had helped stitch which had been hanging on the Graber's clothesline, and Uncle Jerry's bright yellow trash can lid from their house down on the corner, were only two of the objects that Tucker recognized as they spun in the grip of the smaller finger. When he heard the shatter of glass, he knew. Although near darkness had taken over Dunlap and Tucker couldn't see clearly, he knew that the fracturing sound had to be some of the windows in the church, his church, at the end of the road.

Tucker froze and continued to hold onto the doorknob with shaking hands. "I wonder what damage the bigger tornado did?" He stopped and thought of his family still hovering in the basement. Outside, sirens with different, distinct sounds, split the heavy air. Police cars, rescue vehicles, and fire trucks pierced the stillness that had settled in after the wind stood still.

"Tucker," someone called from the backyard.

Tucker looked out into the darkened world of fallen, broken limbs, uprooted bushes, papers from someone's business or home, and Eric Winchester's bent and twisted tricycle from four doors down that lay limp and dirty in Moyers' backyard.

"Tucker," the voice called again from the eerie calmness after the storm passed.

Tucker opened the door. "Who's out there?"

"It's me, Darren Stuart," the voice called back.

As Tucker's eyes adjusted to the darkness, he cautiously stepped outside. Overhead, the stars began to peek through the deadly clouds as they started to dissolve back into the sky. "Are you all okay at your house?"

Mr. Stuart shook his head. "Nothin' like this since 1925. Yeah, we're shaken inside, but we're all fine. Tucker, it's the folks over in Sunnyside who got it real bad. Our generator kicked in to operate my short-wave radio. One of the other operators just reported that the tornadoes have passed, but Midway Trailer Park has been hit hard, and Sunnyside has been flattened. Check on your family, then let's go. They're going to need a lot of help."

Tucker didn't hesitate. "I'll meet you out on Moyer Avenue. I'll be right back." He hurried up a few steps from the summer kitchen to a landing that led to the left down the basement steps. He grabbed ahold of the handrail and bounced down the steps as fast as possible. From the darkness below, he saw the flashlight beaming and heard Gramma reciting a poem she had written as a school girl.

> The footprints I leave behind
> The fingerprints that are mine

> The words that I may say
> May they always stay.

"Is everyone okay?" Tucker hollered. "Gramma, are you okay?"

"Ya, I'm gut." Gramma's shoulders drooped in exhausted relief. "Tucker, where have you been?"

He skipped the details about checking on his Model A, the tepee, and being chased by the tornado fragment. There was no point in worrying her. "Mr. Stuart came to the back door. He said the tornadoes have passed."

"Tornadoes?" Grandpop gasped. "More than one?"

"Yes," Tucker answered as he felt the fear he had experienced, escape him. "A double header took out the trailer park, and a second one hit Sunnyside. Mr. Stuart said those folks are going to need help and asked me to go along."

"Are you sure the dangerous stuff has passed?" Betsy asked. "If it's safe, I can come along and help."

Tucker put his hand on his grandmother's shoulder. "We can all go upstairs now."

Uncle Jacob leaned toward Tucker, and said, "I brought our flashlight down here. I'll bring a couple of those oil lamps out of the basement. That will give us a little light."

"Sure." Tucker followed Uncle Jacob to the tall cabinet in the summer house. Opening the large double doors, he removed some oil lamps that the family had used years before, and in case of an emergency.

Back in the kitchen, his grandparents started through the dark room until Uncle Jacob struck a match and lit the lamps.

Tucker took Betsy's arm and held her back. Glancing at the family as they went into the living room, he whispered, "I'd feel better if you stay here with Gramma and Grandpop. There hasn't been a tornado outbreak in Indiana like this since the 1920s, according to Mr. Stuart. I don't know anything about them. I don't know what to expect."

"Then you stay here, too," Betsy insisted. "If we have no idea what will happen, then you should stay out of danger, too."

"I can't, Bets. Mr. Stuart says we're needed." But, Tucker had no idea how great the need would be.

Chapter Eighteen
SUNNYSIDE

Tucker led the way back through the house. He made sure that his grandparents were safe and comfortable back in their living room. With no electricity, there was no radio or lights. They would have been in the dark without the oil lamps. Gramma was seated safely in her chair when Tucker went out the side door. Joe followed behind before the storm door slammed.

Outside, the grass was strewn with objects the wind blew into the yard. The bright red bird house he had made in the sixth grade no longer hung from the oak limb, but lay broken on the ground, some of the pieces blown to the four corners of Dunlap. His heart ached as he thought about the destruction of Avril Mosher's red barn. Mr. Mosher had his workshop in there along with his milk cows and the few sheep he kept. He'd sheer the woolly animals, and his wife would prepare the wool for thread to make sweaters and socks. Not only was the barn gone, all of the projects and tools to repair them were somewhere in the wind.

Small, twisted twigs and huge branches covered the ground in a dangerous covering. It looked like lattice work that hung on the west facing wall for the honeysuckle to climb on. Each step snapped another piece that would reach up and smack his legs.

"I'm ready," Tucker announced when he met Mr. Stuart on the side street.

The wail of sirens screamed in the air. Emergency vehicles seemed to buzz about in every direction. Cars, loaded with people searching for loved ones, started streaming down the highway. The air was thick with moisture, but strangely, amidst all the destruction and chaos, there was the sweet smell of spring rain. Tucker stopped holding his breath when he saw that Butch Randolf's Sinclair filling station and the grocery next door were still standing. But, what would they find beyond the corner, behind Butch's Sinclair and the fire station that was on County Road 13 just behind the filling station?

Together, Tucker and Mr. Stuart dodged storm debris and oncoming traffic as they darted across the highway. Past the station, they stumbled over litter and lost family treasures that now covered the road and the railroad tracks where Grandpop used to board the train as it slowed down. They focused intently on each step they took, careful not to get their shoes caught between the darkened rails and the wooden ties where slush and mud waited. When Tucker and Mr. Stuart were free from the iron bars, they looked up and stopped in stunned silence.

Tucker strained his eyes and tried to see the many acres beyond the railroad crossing. Why couldn't he see anything?

Where Sunnyside once sprawled out, there was nothing but the rubble from destroyed homes, twisted trees, and the smell of leaking septic tanks. Tucker's chest tightened with sorrow and fear for what they would find, or what would be lost and unable to be found. As the two stumbled down County Road 13, strewn with all types of litter and displaced family treasures, Tucker was shocked. How was he going to be able to know his way around the neighborhood? He knew every street and house, whether it had been painted last spring or if they had installed new gutters last year. Now, he couldn't even find the side streets or the layout of the subdivision. Everything had been ripped up down to the pavement, tossed aside, or blown into a neighborhood miles away.

Downed live electrical lines brought an odor of burning embers from the fires they caused. Some wires sparked and crackled wildly where they lay on the ground.

"Be careful, Tucker," Darren said as he slipped on wet grass and soot-covered gravel near where Klines' house had stood just hours before. "The phone and electrical wires are on the ground. Don't get near any of the downed lines."

Tucker had brought the extra flashlight with him and pointed the beam at a figure by the side of the road. "Mrs. Kline?" He gasped. As he stumbled and scrambled over to her, he slipped and slid on the contents of many homes that lay ankle deep on the ground.

Birdie Kline stood helplessly in front of the wooden floor of what had been her family's home. The beautiful hardwood was covered in slushy trash and water. Tucker knew there would soon be nothing left of the only thing that remained of their home. Water and wood don't go together for very long. Mrs. Kline was bent over in grief and fear. Tucker put his arm around her shoulder. "Mrs. Kline, I am so sorry."

"Tucker ... Harvey ..." she sputtered. "It's Harvey. We headed to the basement but ...." She caught her breath and whispered, "We were just sitting in the living room, eating crackers and the good strawberry jam I bought at the Christmas bazaar a few months back, when we heard the roaring sound. We dashed to the basement. I went down first. Harvey tried to hurry so fast he lost his step and fell. He's hurt, Tucker."

Tucker studied the pile of trash that had once been a comfortable home. He had been in the Kline's house many times. The previous month, Birdie had hosted a Valentine party for the Sunday school class there in her living room. But ... the living room was gone. Nothing remained that bore witness to their lives. He couldn't even find the basement stairs. Where was the basement now? Obviously, it was under the house, but there were no walls, no door. As he stumbled around the destruction, something caught his eye. On the storm-soaked area carpet, near where a wall had previously stood, lay two small stones.

Joe went over and sniffed at the objects. It looked like he had gone into his war-dog training of cautiously searching the area. He nudged the articles with his nose.

Then Tucker remembered. Birdie had created a shadow box and hung it on the wall on the left side of the living room. She was excited to show her Sunday school class when they came in February. There were six little sections in the display. In the first opening was a small manger with a tiny baby laying on some hay Birdie had bought from the Mosher farm months before. In the second box was a little barrel and a small wine glass. She had reminded the class that Jesus's first miracle was at a wedding feast in Cana of Galilee when he turned water into wine. The next little opening was a little pair of glasses, to represent when Jesus made the blind man see. Birdie had laughed and told the class that no glasses were involved, they merely represented the miracle. Next, a man sitting up in a tiny bed told the story of Lazarus being raised from the dead. The fifth box contained an empty cross, indicating how the Roman authorities executed Jesus. And the final display was a hollowed-out rock and a flat stone beside it, telling the world that Jesus had risen from the dead.

Tucker thought his heart would break. Were small, gray stones all that were left of a home where a family was raised and friends came to visit? With his back to Birdie who still waited on the outside ... of nothing, he rubbed his eyes and nose on his coat sleeve. Then, using his flashlight to search the floor for other objects from the shadow box, something shone a little. Beside the stones was a piece of broken mirror, no bigger than one of Gramma's sugar cookies. All the rest of the mirror and frame were gone. He bent over, picked up the piece of glass, wrapped it in his large red handkerchief, and shoved the broken piece and stones into his coat pocket.

"Mrs. Kline." Tucker started slowly so as not to frighten her more. "I've forgotten where the basement steps are." He focused the beam from his flashlight back and forth over broken furniture, smashed and splintered walls, caved in everything. There was nothing more left that looked like a house.

Joe walked aimlessly. Without a command, he too was left to wander through the rubble.

Birdie looked at the empty space, full of nothing, yet full of everything, put her hands over her eyes, and sobbed. She tried to catch her breath and whispered, "I'll find the basement stairs. Let me get in there."

"Mrs. Kline, no." Tucker tried to help. He wanted to comfort her, but he didn't know what to do or what to say. "The only thing I can do to help you is dig through all of this." He wished he had special words that would have helped. But all he could do, was … do. "Let me and Mr. Stuart bring Harvey up out of the basement."

"No, Tucker," she gasped. "I have to pull myself together." She stood up, then straightened as tall as she could. "Ah … the basement steps are in the center of the house." She reached for Tucker's hand and gave in. "I promise to wait right here, if you and Darren can bring my Harvey out of there, Tucker."

"Joe," Tucker bent low and spoke with authority, "find the basement steps. Find Mr. Kline."

Joe rubbed his nose on Mrs. Kline's skirt and began snorting his way through the debris.

Tucker's voice cracked a little as he handed Birdie the two stones. "I found these," he choked out the words.

Mrs. Kline took the stones in her hands and held them close to her body. Tucker wondered if she was afraid to lose the only thing he could find. "Oh, Tucker," she whispered, "thank you."

"I also found this," he said handing her the piece of broken mirror. "I think you told us that it was your grandmother's mirror."

She stared at the broken mirror and shook her head. Taking the piece in her hands, she murmured, "I don't have to see what's been. I'll have to look toward tomorrow."

Chapter Nineteen
HELPING HARVEY

Tucker knew he had to help the Klines but didn't know where to begin. Saving someone trapped in a collapsed house was more than putting up a tepee.

Mrs. Kline smiled weakly at Tucker, held the stones close, and whispered, "Please, get Harvey out of there."

Darren Stuart patted her shoulder. "Try not to worry, Birdie. Tucker and I can do it. You stay here," he pointed insistently to the edge of the road. "Come on, Tucker."

They wound their way through all of the rubble of a house, most completely blown away, and some left in tiny pieces by the mighty force of wind. Tucker pushed pieces of an upturned, heavy living room couch out of the way. Under many feet of boards and trash, they found the top of the dining room table. It was still right-side up but missed all of its legs. Oddly, the maple finish was still spotless. In sloppy, dirty water, ripped curtains and all the elements that make a house a home were piled and tangled in what had been the room where her family had gathered at the end of the day.

"Joe." Tucker bent and rubbed the German shepherd behind his ears. "You earned a Silver Star for bravery and the Purple Heart in the war. Now, I need you to find Harvey. Joe, go find Harvey."

Joe sniffed around under all the damage, then stopped, sat down, and stared at a single spot.

"Over here!" Tucker shouted. "Joe found the steps!" The walls and basement door were gone, only a gaping hole in the floor remained, where dirty storm water gushed in. "Mr. Kline? Harvey?" Tucker shouted into the blackness under the house. Wrapping his arms around his dog's neck, he gave him a big bear hug. "Good boy, Joe."

"Here," a crackling, weak voice came from down under the destruction. "I'm here. I think my leg is broken."

Tucker pointed the flashlight into the old opening that resembled a well and cast a beam into the darkness. "I see you, Mr. Kline. Can you follow the light and walk over to the steps? Can you move at all?"

"I'll try," he agreed weakly. "Oh!" he winced in pain. Each word sounded harder to speak than the last. He finally added, "I limped a little, but I don't think I can get up the steps. The light helps. I can see the stairs …," he moaned. "They're right there."

"I'll go down," Mr. Stuart offered boldly. "Tucker, you hold the flashlight past me and shine it on Harvey." Tucker cautiously balanced his feet on the wet top step.

Darren carefully descended the steps made slick and slimy by the dripping rainwater and everything else that floated in the storm's gush. Once he got to the bottom of the stairs, he leaned over and grabbed Harvey up under his arm. "What do you think, Harvey? Do you know if you could try?"

Huffing in pain, Harvey still managed to joke, "I'll probably complain, or yell in your ear, Darren. But I don't plan to stay in this open-air basement forever."

Tucker laid down on his stomach in dirty water and globs of something that looked like Birdie's jelly that floated by. From there, he could direct the flashlight and be prepared to grab Harvey's hand when he got close enough to the surface. "I'm right here, Mr. Kline."

Darren wrapped his hand under Harvey's arm. "When you're ready, we'll start up. I'll warn you ahead of time, this might be very painful. But you have to get out of here." Slowly, they started up the steps.

"Wait," Tucker shouted when he saw the pain on Harvey's face. "Mr. Kline, I just remembered. Turn around and sit down on the steps. Then, you can come up, one tread at a time, pushing yourself up by your hands and arms to sit on the next step. It's just like you probably did when you were a kid."

Darren chuckled. "Tucker, you are brilliant."

Mr. Kline plopped down on the second step and took a deep breath. Slowly, he raised himself up backward by the strength in his arms. When he finally got to the top step, which was the floor of what had been the kitchen, he stopped and panted, waiting to regain some strength to stand up.

"Okay, Harvey," Darren began. "I'll come around you." Mr. Stuart stepped out of the pit of the basement and carefully slipped past the man who had collapsed on the top step.

"I can get Mr. Kline under one arm," Tucker said as he pulled himself up from the floor, his clothes dripping.

"And I'll support him under the other arm," Mr. Stuart said as he bent to wrap his arms around Harvey.

Tucker stooped and slipped his arm under Mr. Kline's shoulder. He watched Darren for a small nod. He figured it would be best to pull Harvey up without warning. There was no need for him to anticipate pain. On Mr. Stuart's signal, together, they pulled Harvey up onto his feet.

He limped and stumbled, his face distorted in pain. "Thanks guys. I thank the Lord we had a basement, and I thank Him again for getting out of that basement."

"Oh, Harvey," Birdie cried as she saw Tucker and Darren bring her husband to the edge of the property line. She fell into Harvey's arms. "Thank you, thank you," she said and hugged Tucker, then gave Darren a side hug.

"Can you get him to the hospital yourself, Birdie?" Mr. Stuart asked as he looked around for what might have been her car.

She searched the property with an empty stare, then gasped. "Look," she said and pointed. "The house is gone but the garage out back is still standing." Reaching for Tucker's arm, she said, "There's a second set of keys in the glove compartment, Tucker. Go back there and …" she looked at the yard, covered in scraps and trash from half the houses that used to be her neighbors' homes. "I don't know. You'll have to drive it through the yard, trying to find the driveway, and hope you don't run over any nails." She looked at Mr. Stuart. "Darren, please, you can help Harvey stand here while Tucker drives the car up. It's alright. Everyone knows he's fourteen but drives his Model A everywhere."

"Birdie," Darren said softly, "it's an emergency. I've never heard that Tucker has had an accident or a ticket. It'll be fine."

As he tried to get to the back of the property, Tucker felt like he was on an expedition into the Amazon rain forest, pushing and pulling house parts and fallen tree limbs out of the way. Off to the left, the yard was covered with the roof from someone's garage or shed. That afternoon, there had been a paved driveway from the garage to the street. It was now buried. He tried to push and pull as much of the small bits and pieces of the Kline family's life out of the way as he could. Something sticky clung to the bottom of his shoe. Using a piece of rock that had been part of the footpath from the house to the garage, he scrapped the bottom of his shoe. At that point, Tucker wasn't concerned about dirty shoes. His main thought was not letting the glob under his shoe cause him to fall.

He pulled the garage doors apart and found Kline's bright red 1941 Mercury car sitting inside without a speck of dust on it. The garden tools still hung on the walls by the special metal brackets Harvey had bought to organize his garage. Nothing had moved ... except for the disappearance of the entire house a few yards away. Tucker got in the car and hoped the Kline's had replaced the second set of keys as they had planned. Lesson learned, same lesson another vital example. Put things back where they belong.

He got in the car and nervously searched the glove compartment. *Thank you, Lord,* he whispered. With the key in the ignition, he pulled out of the single car garage. Driving cautiously, he zig-zagged through what had been the backyard, where a child's swing had stood, and Birdie had brought out her large flower pots to clean and get them ready for spring flowers. All were broken or simply gone. The crackle and pop from under the tires seemed to announce a final destruction of the "things" of life. The F4 tornado had stolen it all.

When Tucker got to the front of the property, he turned off the engine and jumped out of the car. "Okay, let's get him inside."

Harvey's pain was obvious, as his face twitched tightly. He sat down on the passenger seat and stared at Tucker.

"I'll hold your broken right leg," Tucker offered. "You turn and get that left one in."

"Thanks, Tucker." Mr. Kline tried to twist his face into a smile. "You'll have to get my leg in the car, or it'll drag on the road all the way to the hospital. That won't be good."

Tucker was glad to hear that Mr. Kline was able to joke a little. "That doesn't sound very safe or comfortable." As carefully as possible, Tucker swung Harvey's leg into the car. Tucker winced as he saw Mr. Kline struggle.

Once Harvey was in, Birdie was ready to leave, but she couldn't move. She clung to the steering wheel and started crying again. Tucker leaned in the window.

"Are you okay?" he whispered so not to upset her injured husband.

"I don't have a purse or a driver's license, Tucker," she sobbed. "I'll have to drive right through the middle of Elkhart with no ID."

"You'll be fine, Mrs. Kline." Tucker assured her in his upbeat way. "I don't have a driver's license either."

Her smile looked tired, but she always greeted whatever came her way with a smile. "Tucker, remember, these are the 'after-days,' between the 'before,' and the 'heart-filling miracles.' Tucker, we've seen one miracle already. You saved my Harvey." Birdie had to stop as the words stuck in her throat. After a few seconds, she said, "I'll see you Sunday." She pulled out onto the litter covered space that had been the road just hours before.

"I'll see you Sunday," Tucker echoed and thought about "the miracle." He watched her cautiously drive through the sad remains of the storm and wondered if she would be able to take care of Harvey and still be in church on Easter?

Chapter Twenty
JOE TO THE RESCUE

The tornadoes started going through Dunlap about 6:30 p.m. that Palm Sunday. At 8:30, Tucker and Mr. Stuart were still searching everywhere with Tucker's flashlight and the bright twinkle from the stars that had finally come out. The gift of the tiny lights in the sky seemed to promise that God would bless their service of searching.

When Tucker was able to catch his breath and look around the destroyed neighborhood, he saw that members of the Dunlap Volunteer Fire Department were working in the area, too. Many of members were Tucker's cousins. They had set up their search beacons to help in the recovery process. The department and many community friends and neighbors were helping search for trapped survivors. Tucker kept praying they would all be found in time.

Timbers, furniture, overturned cars, downed trees, fallen walls, and caved in roofs were all cast aside like upturned trash cans at each small plot where a home once stood. They slowly had to search so as not to miss anything, when the urge was to quickly find anyone who had fallen.

"Tucker!" Vinny shouted as he ran toward them. Gus was behind him a few steps, puffing and hurrying to keep up. "They don't answer the phone at Morty's house."

"Morty?" Tucker thought of all the problems the bully had caused over the last few years. Still, no one deserved to be trapped under garbage. Then he remembered Morty's help the month before, and his heart softened. "Where does he live?"

Vinny shrugged in anxious bewilderment. "I don't know. I can't make anything out. The streets are gone, the houses are flattened."

Mr. Stuart took Vinny by both shoulders and spoke with gentle confidence. "Location of Morty's house. How many streets down from the highway was it before the tornado took it away?"

"Hey guys, how can I help," Morty offered as he ran up. To Tucker, he looked the same, but there was a change in Morty Kingman.

"Morty?" Vinny gasped. "We were worried."

Tucker couldn't believe it. There he stood. "Morty? Where have you been? There was no answer on the telephone at your house."

"We were visiting my grandparents in Elkhart." Morty eyes were large, and he jittered up and down. "We heard about the tornadoes on the radio. We hurried home to check on our house and the neighborhood."

Darren raised his hand in praise. "Praise the Lord that you're all okay. Was your house destroyed?"

"Oddly, no," Morty said in amazement. "The garage is trashed, and it looks like the gutters on the roof of the house may have been damaged. Like everyone, we have no electricity. But the house itself seems to be okay. The house next door is leveled, and, we can't find Melrose."

Tucker raised the corner of his mouth. "Melrose?"

"He's our new puppy." Morty wrung his hands and paced. "He's such a sweet little puppy."

Tucker asked, "Where was he before you all left for Elkhart?"

"Um." Morty thought as his eyes grew large. "He was outside. I whistled for him to come in, but he wouldn't come before we left for Elkhart. The yard was fenced, and it was a beautiful afternoon, so we let him stay outside." Tears filled his eyes.

"Let's go look." Tucker squeezed Morty's shoulder and started walking. "Maybe he found a place to hide."

What would have been approximately two streets over, and on the other side of the road, they found a street that had nearly been passed over. Trees were downed but managed to fall away from the houses. Many of the houses looked safe from the terrible storm.

Morty turned down that second street and ran over to a brick house, the third from the corner. "Melrose!"

Many dogs barked in the distance. Tucker strained to listen, but none had the yappy sound of a puppy.

Morty lifted boards that lay in the yard from the oak planks his father had stacked near the garage. "Dad said he was going to build a dog house for Melrose. It was going to be a real fancy one that had a dog door into the house on the right side." Monty looked under the fallen clothespin bag his mom had left hanging on the line. The bag lay in a heap over by the pole that the wash lines had been strung on. The lines were gone. "The clothes lines might be in Illinois by now." Then Morty's eyes had a glisten of memory as he whispered, "The puppy likes small, cozy places."

Tucker slipped his fingers through Joe's collar. "Joe, find the puppy, the little dog."

Joe sniffed around the old turned-over rain barrel that now lay broken on the ground. No little dog. He turned up his nose and sniffed the air. Like a flash, he turned, darted into the collapsed end of the garage, and came out carrying an old metal bird cage in his mouth. Inside, was a small, black, curly-haired poodle.

"Melrose!" Morty yelled and took the cage from Joe's mouth. "Melrose, how did you get in there?"

Mr. Stuart laughed and rubbed the puppy's head. "You said Melrose likes cozy places. He probably felt safe inside the bird cage."

Tucker laughed. "I would have felt a little caged in."

Chapter Twenty-One
THE TEAPOT

Tucker and the others were covered in the storm's debris. He felt wet, cold, and sticky. When Mrs. Crammer wandered over, he couldn't help but stop. She had sung in the choir and had been at their house for the quilting bee many times. But, this time, Tucker hardly recognized her. Her eyes were vacant, like there was no light behind them.

"Have you seen it, Tucker?" she asked while scanning the bits and pieces of her house but seemed to see nothing.

"What, Mrs. Crammer? What are you looking for?"

"Mama's pretty teapot," she whispered listlessly.

"A teapot?" Tucker asked, looking around at a house completely destroyed. "No ma'am, I haven't seen it." He gently took her by the arm. "You better get out of all of this."

"No." She pulled her arm away. "Momma is gone now. The teapot is the only thing I have of hers."

"Yes, Ma'am, I understand," Tucker said as he thought about the foot tall white, cement rabbit that Gramma used as a door stop.

When his mother was a young child, she had helped the masons rebuild the front steps by staying out of their way. They molded a rabbit for her out of the leftover concrete. It was all Tucker had of his mother, too.

"Do you really understand?" she asked and perked up a little. "The teapot was in the china cabinet in the dinning room. Do you think you and your friends could find the cabinet?"

"We'll try," Gus answered and started into the trash pile of her destroyed home.

"Where was the dining room?" Tucker asked as he stumbled through the piles of rubbish. Tucker thought, *The whole house could be in Goshen by now. Or broken into a million pieces.*

Mrs. Crammer put both hands to her temples and rubbed as if it would help her to remember. Pointing to the left, she said, "The dining room was over there." Tucker thought he heard hope in her voice.

Gus and Morty hurried over to the west side of the trash pile. Vinny followed, but Tucker felt tired, like his legs weighed ten pounds each. He trudged through all the brokenness and wondered how a china teapot could survive a wind of 200 to 250 miles per hour.

"Over here!" Morty called out.

What? How could it be?

The boys all gathered around what might have been a Mahogany, bow front, Hepplewhite china cabinet [9]. Tucker recognized it because he had gone with Aunt

Cora, Luke, and Uncle Jerry to Goshen's Kinsbury Furniture Store, when Cora was looking for one. She talked unendingly about it and described every detail a multitude of times. The one she found first was too expensive for them, but the store owner just happen to have a smaller, used, similar hutch that had recently come back to the store.

The cabinet in the spot that had been Crammer's dining room was partially there but shattered. The drawers and the bottom of the cabinet were broken and splintered on the wet floor. Special, hand embroidered cream-colored napkins lay, nearly unrecognizable, in the filth on the floor, except for the pattern like Gramma liked to sew.

The glass in the upper section was shattered. Tucker couldn't even find any evidence of it ever having been in the door.

Tucker stopped, and his breath caught in his throat. There was a corner of the upper shelves still intact. "Come on, guys. Help me separate the splinters from the possibility."

The three friends joined Tucker and carefully got ahold of the corner of the piece of the cabinet that was left. It was upside down and laid across the dining room drapes. They reminded Tucker of the floor-length, pinch-pleated drapes made of something called barkcloth that Gramma had made for Uncle David and Aunt Karen when they moved into their new parsonage in Elkhart. Tucker figured the drapes had been floral, but they were buried so deep, and were drowned in so much dirt and slime, it was hard to tell.

"Careful guys," Tucker cautioned.

Slowly, they got under the remaining corner and pulled it off the drapery. There, in the mud and shards from broken, family heirloom dishes, Tucker lifted the handle of a fancy, blue and yellow teapot. It was stuffed around by the soggy drapes, like a protective blanket, intended to shield it from the trash.

"Mrs. Crammer," Tucker turned slowly, "I think I have it. Is it blue?"

"Yes, yes, Tucker, blue." She trudged a few steps into the mess before Mr. Stuart stopped her.

"No, Gilda. It's too dangerous to walk in there." Darren put his arm around her waist to comfort her and remind her to stay out of what had been her home.

"Here, Mrs. Crammer." Tucker handed over the pot and wondered how a miracle like that could happen.

"I knew you would find it, Tucker." Mrs. Crammer held the teapot close with her right hand and patted Tucker's chest with the other. "You're a good boy."

"Mother!" Gilda's daughter, Velma, shouted from the trash covered street. "I was so worried."

"I'm sorry. I was so flustered and had no phone." Gilda waved the teapot over her head. "Tucker found your grandma's teapot."

"Come on, Mother. You come to my house."

Tucker smiled. Another after-day miracle. He was beginning to understand. To recognize the blessing, you have to be willing to accept the blessing God sends and not be disappointed that your order hasn't been filled.

Chapter Twenty-Two
SAFE IN THE BATHTUB

"Barbara!" Steven Beiler yelled into the collapsed remains of his home. "Stevie! Becky!"

"Mr. Beiler," Tucker soothed with his hand to the man's shoulder. "Do you need help?"

"My wife, Barbara, was at home with the children while I ran into the office." He bent in surrender to overwhelming fear. "There's nothing left."

Tucker flashed his light over the nothingness and destruction that was left of the Beiler home. "I don't see anything," he said. He wished he could report they were found, that the Beiler family was hiding under the dining room table. But there was no dining room and there was no table. All Tucker could see was ripped pieces of dry wall, still covered in dirty, and soaked, blue striped wallpaper. There wasn't even enough pieces to reach from the floor to halfway to the ceiling.

"They were right here!" Beiler demanded as he pointed into the darkness of the night. "I wouldn't have left if I had known. The stuff at the office was just that, stuff. My family was here."

"What is it, Steven?" Mr. Stuart asked as he came over from helping Gilda Crammer get safely into her daughter's car. "How can we help?"

"My family was right here, at home," he said again and started sobbing as he fell to his knees in the filth and trash. Choking through his tears, he repeated, "I know, they were right here."

"Okay," Darren stated flatly, "Tucker, the boys, and I will find them." He looked around the frantic survival area. He pointed to some first responders at the destroyed house next door. "Gary," he hollered. "Shine your spotlight over here."

"Sure. Darren, is that you?" Gary shouted.

"It is," he said and laughed. "It's hard to tell in all this debris."

Gary Armstrong directed the beam of his spotlight onto the rubbish of the Beiler home. The light scanned slowly left then right, front then back.

All of them searched the space as the beam cast the light slowly, roaming from side to side. Beiler's fancy Baldwin console piano Barbara had just bought the month before lay broken in half. Part of it was there, but the other piece, the lower notes below middle C were nowhere.

"Wait!" Tucker shouted. "Go back."

Gary set the beam back a couple of feet. "What is it?" Gary squinted into the dust of the night. "I don't see anything."

Steven stood up and blinked desperately. "It's the bathroom." He strained to see. "Yes, all of those walls have fallen in on the area where the bathroom was."

"Let's see what we can do," Tucker offered and started toward the center right of the house.

Ceiling beams, yellow plastered walls, a window frame with broken glass all lay across the bathroom door. The living room sofa had been flipped over and thrown against that wall, along with broken pieces of chairs and items that couldn't even be identified.

"Barbara!" Steven shouted.

"Shh," Tucker hushed. "Listen," he whispered.

"Daddy," a small voice cried from the other side of the barrier.

"I'm here, Becky," Steven called out as he fell into the trash heap.

"Wait, Steven," Darren cautioned. "Let's handle this properly. There's a lot of glass in there, boys. Be careful. If you have gloves, put them on."

"I don't have any." Tucker pulled his jacket pockets inside out.

"I do." Morty offered and he slipped one of the leather driving gloves on.

"You could ruin those nice gloves," Darren warned him. "The glass can shred that leather."

"Daddy, Daddy," the little girl's voice called.

Tucker couldn't believe his eyes. Of all the things Morty had done, he was changing. Morty seemed to melt right in front of him.

"That's okay," Morty said as he looked down at his gloves. "It sounds like the little one is worth it."

Was that Morty talking? I've never heard him care about anything except himself.

"I'll move the big pieces of glass," Morty offered. "You guys get the rest of the stuff."

"Keep the light on this spot, Gary," Darren indicated, like the director of a short movie. "We've found the family."

Together, they pulled the smaller pieces of the window frame off and threw them to the side. "Okay, a couple of you get ahold of the sofa and let's flip it over there." Tucker took one end and Vinny the other. They set it aside as if it were a new piece of fine furniture.

Each grabbed broken pieces of long, sleek dining room chair legs, broken lamps, the pieces and fragments of dry wall, and bits and pieces of the rest of the house. Last, they had two large beams to tackle.

Since the ceiling was extra high, twelve-feet, the beams were eight inches by ten inches wide and twenty feet long in the living room. It was two of those beams that now pressed against the bathroom door. One lay across the other and would have to be moved carefully so as not to have them slip and trip one of the rescuers.

Morty, Gus, and Vinny took one end of the first beam. Tucker and Mr. Stuart were on the other end. Tucker gave the order. "On three, hoist the beam. One … two … three." Together, they yanked the wooden beam from where it lay in front of the door, and set it aside.

"One more," Mr. Stuart announced. "Take position." He waited while the boys stretched and prepared to deadlift the last beam. "Ready? One … two … three." Again, they lifted the huge lumber and swung it off to the side.

Steven Beiler stepped into what was left of his home and grabbed the doorknob of the only room in the house left partially standing, and jerked it open. "Barbara!" Steven yelled when he saw his wife slumped in the bathtub, unconscious. Becky reached up for him, and little Stevie had his arms wrapped around his mommy.

"Here, Becky," Tucker offered calmly. "Let me help you out of the tub." He pulled her out of the bathtub and held the four-year-old close. He had never babysat a day in his life. But, he had played with some of his little cousins, and spending the morning with Micky had been a good rehearsal.

"Come on, Stevie," Gus spoke softly and calmly to the two-year-old. "Let me hold you so your daddy can help your momma." He reached down, like an experienced babysitter, took the boy in his arms, and helped him out of the way. "I have two little sisters," he explained.

"Barbara." Steven patted her face gently, frantically. "Babs? Wake up, Honey. Open your eyes. The tornado has passed."

Barbara's eyes opened slightly, and a faint smile crossed her lips. She touched the top of her head and winced. "Ouch. I think the shower door hit me in the head."

"You got the children down into the tub. Barbara, that was perfect," Steven said as he pulled her into his arms. "You saved them."

Mr. Stuart reached down and helped Steve get his wife out of the bathtub and set her safely on the floor.

Barbara swayed as she stood there a minute and grabbed Steven's arm. "I feel woozy."

"Steve, you need to get her to the hospital," Darren cautioned. "Maybe you can find someone to stay with the children while you're in the Emergency Room."

"No!" Becky insisted. "I want to stay with Mama."

"I'll call Barbara's mom and dad from the hospital. I hope Elkhart still has telephone service." Steve wrapped his arms around his wife. "They can meet us at the hospital. Gracie can entertain the children in the waiting room while Barbara receives treatment."

"Morty," Vinny directed, "let's clear a little path so everyone is safe getting out of here." Quickly, they pulled and kicked unrecognizable pieces of something or globs of nothing that cluttered the floor, and tossed them off to the side.

Tucker carried Becky to her daddy's car, followed by Gus with little Stevie. They placed them in the back seat. "Now, stay seated," Tucker cautioned. "Your daddy is so happy you are all okay, it might rattle his driving if you stand up behind him. He will want to get to the hospital as soon as he can with no distractions."

"Okay, Tucker." Becky patted his face as he leaned close. "Can I come to your house sometime?"

Tucker was surprised. "You sure can. If your parents have time this week, once your mom feels better, they can bring you by. I have something special in the orchard I bet you'll enjoy seeing."

He closed the door and stepped out of the way so Steve to get Barbara in. Once she was safely placed in the front passenger seat of his new, four-door DeSoto

Deluxe/Suburban car, he kissed her sore forehead and patted her cheek. "I love you, Honey." He hurried around the back of the car and safely pull out of the landfill that was now their neighborhood.

Chapter Twenty-Three
ADAM'S CRAYONS

Velma loaded her mother in the car just as the Beiler car pulled away. "Thank you, Tucker," Velma sighed. "What you and your friends did for Mother meant a lot to her."

Tucker smiled and helped Velma come around the car safely and leave. But there was more. Everywhere he looked, there were people sobbing or walking around in a mental stupor, unable to make sense out of any of it.

"Tucker," six-year-old Adam Campbell called out as he came up. "Have you seen my new box of crayons?"

"Crayons, Adam? No, no crayons." Tucker wished he could smell the familiar fragrance of crayons and sit on the floor and fill a coloring book. The odor that was drowning him at the moment was the open septic tank at the back of Campbell's property. Tucker had no idea how the tornado had been able to dig up a corner of the septic system. It was underground. He didn't have to understand. Nothing seemed to make sense that evening.

"But Momma just bought the crayons for me when she picked up the ham at the grocery store yesterday."

He looked at the spot where his two story, colonial style home had stood. "I haven't even opened the box yet."

"Where's your mother, son?" Mr. Stuart stooped down to Adam's level and put his arm around the boy's shoulder.

"Um…" Adam looked around, empty, alone. "I don't know." He sat down on a wet rock that might have been placed at the end of their driveway. "I'll wait here."

"This isn't the best place to wait." Tucker pointed to a rescue truck that came around the corner. "They wouldn't see you down here. You could get hit."

"But, I'm not allowed to go anywhere without letting Momma know." He looked into the void where his house had been. "I know my crayons are in there somewhere."

Tucker squatted down to Adam's level and knelt in the aftermath of the storm. He knew that Sargent Campbell had been killed in WWII. Adam's mother was all the boy had. Where was she? He asked casually to not alarm him, "Did your mother say she was going someplace?"

"I don't remember." Adam's words drifted off into nothingness.

"Okay. Did she need something from the grocery?"

"I don't know," he muttered. "Oh, she said she was going to pick up some ice cream. I was playing next door." He looked into the void that had been his friend's house. "But, the big wind came, and we went to the basement. I climbed out first."

"Did she go into the ice cream shop in Elkhart, Wray's Ice Cream?" Tucker suddenly realized where Mrs. Campbell was.

"Yes, the big one on that side of the street." He pointed to the left. "I like the chocolate ice cream from there." Adam didn't move.

Suddenly it all began to make sense. "Have you seen your neighbors since they came out of the basement?" Tucker hoped he wouldn't find someone else trapped below.

"No, not yet." Adam looked in the direction of his friend's house. "But they have a living room down there."

"Adam, I think I know where your mother is. Some nice men from the Army are here, helping to direct traffic."

"The Army? My daddy was in the Army." Adam perked up when Tucker mentioned friends of his dad.

"And, it takes longer to get home, with all the cars trying to find loved ones." Tucker looked up at the dark sky with a bit of star light peeking through. "I have an idea." He took Adam's small hand in his. "How would you like to be a rescue worker?"

"A rescue worker?' The boy brightened and jumped up. "Wow! Sure I would."

"You come and show me where the house was that your friends lived in. We can rescue them together." Tucker motioned for the others to follow. He watched as Adam slipped on his first few steps away from his rock-seat. "Would you like to ride on Joe's back?" Tucker asked. "You could keep your feet dry up higher."

"Sure. I'd be like a Cavalry rider. My mother read a book to me about the old west and the men who patrolled there." Adam let Tucker lift him onto Joe's back. "Okay, let's see." Adam pointed to the area that would have been his backyard. "That way, Joe."

Tucker spoke softly, "Take it easy, Joe. You have an inexperienced rider on your back."

"Hey," Adam complained. "I've ridden a horse on the Merry-Go-Round at the Elkhart County Fair."

"Oh, pardon me," Tucker said and smiled. "I should have thought of that."

Gus, Morty, and Vinny trotted along in a special step mimicking a prancing horse. Tucker rolled his eyes and laughed. He had never seen the three in any kind of a playful mood. Maybe the tornado blew through, from one ear and out the other and changed their way of thinking. *Maybe something good has come from the storm.*

Joe carried Adam through the backyard, across the gritty, roofing shingles that lay where they fell when the wind jerked them up and dumped them on the ground.

"There's Momma's tennis racket," Adam pointed to a mangled racket that bore no resemblance to a bat for hitting tennis balls.

Tucker studied the twisted shape. "How did you recognize it?"

"Momma took my old crayons and drew my face on the strings." He looked back and pointed again. "See the brown hair? Just like me. Some of the crayons broke while she was drawing. She promised to get me a new box. That's what I am looking for."

They made their way carefully through the side yard of the house that used to be behind Adam's. Then crossed the street in front of the property.

There was nothing left of the home that had stood there. Yet, a wooden swing still hung from a tree branch just inside the property line. Potted spring flowers that had just started blooming, where still in their pots. The house was gone.

Adam's bottom lip began to quiver. "The house used to be right here. See, there's Jacky Jone's picture on the wall."

Out of the structure of the whole house, there was only one partial wall standing. The picture of Adam's friend Jacky was still smiling from the wreckage.

"Come on," Adam ordered and tried to slide down off Joe's back.

"Here," Gus offered. "Let me help you."

Tucker was amazed and pleased by Gus's change in personality. If he could have had brain surgery to insert a kindness button, Tucker would not have been surprised. Gus was now caring and gentle, when months before, he had been a bully and a thug.

Adam slipped away from Tucker and dodged all the litter until he came to the hole in the floor called the basement steps. Leaning into the hole, he hollered, "Jacky? Are you in there?"

"Adam?" a young voice called from below. "Where did you go?"

Looking down into the basement, Tucker saw another small face. "Hi, Jacky. I'm Tucker McBride."

"I know you." Jacky laughed. "You sometimes pump gas for my dad. And, you always remember my favorite kind of candy bar when we go inside the station."

Tucker smiled and shined the flashlight on Jacky's face. "I remember you. You like the Baby Ruth candy bar. Are your parents down there with you?"

"Yes," a deep voice answered. "Connie and I are here with Jacky and our daughter, Peggy. We're okay. We have a bathroom and a little kitchen area. We'll be fine until the insurance office opens tomorrow."

"Good," Mr. Stuart added. "So, no one is hurt?"

"We are all fine." Mr. Jones sounded confident but tired. "We're just shaken and hoping that it doesn't rain tonight. We're also on guard for stray animals that might want to get in."

"Good." Mr. Stuart invited, "If you need a place to wait it out, Albert Finny just told me that the survivors are going to the church. I'm glad you are all okay."

"If you find something that will work, you can cover the opening so it doesn't rain in," Jacky's father asked but he sounded cautious. "Just make sure you mark it real good so we can be found again."

Tucker pointed his flashlight at Mr. Jones. "Do you have food down there?" It was widely known that food was often on Tucker's mind.

"Yes, and possibly," he answered slowly. "With no electricity, we can't cook any meat. We just had Whistlers deliver a half of a beef. It's in the freezer and should stay frozen, even with the electricity off, for twenty-four hours with the door kept closed. Connie canned a lot of fruit and vegetables. We can eat fruit for a day. If the electricity doesn't come back on tomorrow, I'll have to see about moving everything in the freezer to Roberts's Community Freezer."

"If you want a good hot meal tomorrow, come over to the church," Mr. Stuart offered.

"Adam," a female voice shrieked from the side road.

"I'm here, Mama," Adam yelled in glee. "I'm over here at Jacky's house, or ... basement."

"Over here, Mrs. Campbell," Tucker called. A great sigh escaped him and a peace took over. A boy had found his mother.

Chapter Twenty-Four
CHECKING IN

Mr. Stuart rubbed dirt from his brow and coughed. "Like I told the others, Albert Finley just stopped and told me they are setting up a shelter at the church for the survivors. They'll need all kinds of things tonight: blankets, water, food, and who-knows-what. Maybe they need our help there now."

Mr. Stuart, Tucker, and the fabled *bullies-three* all headed back toward the church. With more rescue equipment in the area, there were more spot lights. The area Tucker and the others had been working in was now visible, and heart-breaking. There were still so many people in need of rescue, Tucker left reluctantly. He first stopped at home.

"Gramma?" he called as he entered the side door. The flicker and scent of lamps came from the front of the house. Tucker felt warmed by the flames.

The three boys were behind him. Dirt from their shoes cluttered their path through the house.

A soft glow from glass oil lamps that had lit the house so many years ago, now filled the living room again. His grandmother was back in her rocker, with her crocheting in her lap, and a wick burning brightly in the lamp on the table beside her.

"Gus, Morty, and I will stay over near the door, Mrs. Moyer," Vinny offered apologetically. "Our shoes are covered in dirt and slime."

"Good thinking, Vinny," Gramma responded as her sigh revealed her relief. "It can all be cleaned up."

Tucker's grandparents were used to adjusting to whatever came their way. A catastrophe wasn't taken as someone's fault, and they certainly didn't blame God. It was life. And when things happened that interrupted their routine, their routine was no longer routine.

"Tucker, you're home," she sighed with relief. "You've been gone for hours." She looked up from her hand-work with a tired, strained expression on her face. "Ah, Vincent, it's good to see you again."

"Yes, Ma'am." Vinny smiled. He had grown close to Tucker's grandmother since she coerced him into coming to church.

"Sorry I was out so long, Gramma. We helped several families. It was a hard evening." He stopped in mid-thought. "But it was really special, too," he said as he continued through the house. "Can I take some peanut butter sandwiches over to the church? Mr. Stuart and I have been helping to search for people trapped in the mess where their house used to be. We just pulled out Birdie Kline's husband."

"Oh, my goodness," she gasped. "Is Harvey alright?"

"Yeah ... sorta." He stopped and explained. "He has a broken leg, but, other than that, he's okay."

"Praise the Lord. I will pray for him," Gramma assured him. Then, remembering the PBJ's, she said, "Ja, of course." She started to get up. "So you're going over now?"

"Mr. Stuart, Gus, Morty, Vinny, and I are going over to the church to help set it up for survivors. We're going to see what we can do to help."

Gramma's hand flew to her mouth. "Oh, Tucker, it sounds bad out there."

"A lot of houses were damaged or destroyed." Tucker stopped and wrapped his arms around his grandmother like he did when he was little. "There will be a lot of people looking for a place to get inside, while they think about their next step."

He went into the kitchen and pulled bread from the bread box, a jar of Skippy from the cupboard, and a jar of Gramma's special strawberry jam from the refrigerator. Tucker smiled. He could live on those three ingredients for days.

"Oh my. Let me help you," she offered. She pulled a butter knife from the drawer and prepared to spread goodness on slices of homemade bread.

"Did you say they're setting up a shelter in the church?" Grandpop asked as he walked into the dark kitchen carrying one of the table lamps. "Maybe I'd better go over and check on things. They'll need to know where I store the toilet paper, Dixie cups, and paper plates. It'll be dark over there, too. There are a lot of candles in the church's basement."

Uncle Jacob had been carrying the home flashlight around with him. "I'll check on our yard and what I can see of the house. You did well, Tucker," he added. "You knew we'd need light. I'm glad you picked up our extra batteries earlier."

Gramma added a generous helping of dessert to the quick meal. "I made lemon sugar cookies yesterday. Only a few were eaten last evening." She pulled the cookie crock from under the counter. "Tucker, you take them over, crock and all. We can get the container when it needs filling again."

"Sure, Gramma." With his grandmother's help, he finished making the sandwiches, wrapped them each in wax paper, and started to balance the sandwiches on top of the crock. He hoped his balancing act would get it all across the street safely.

Vinny reached for the PBJ sandwiches. "I'll carry those for you," he offered.

Out on Moyer Avenue, Mr. Stuart hustled along after Tucker as he crossed the street. "I checked on my family. Do you need help with that crock?"

"No, thanks. I have it." When they got to the church steps, Tucker nodded over to the Stuarts' house. "Are they okay? Does your family need anything?"

Mr. Stuart chuckled lightly. "Nothing that a little electricity wouldn't cure."

Tucker took the flashlight out of his pocket and beamed the light on the steps. "I agree with that."

Chapter Twenty-Five
THE ENTERTAINER

Over at the church, Tucker had followed his grandfather through the halls and into every cabinet and closet since he was three years old. He remembered the first time Gramma suggested that Grandpop take him along for a quick walk through.

As they left the house that day, Grandpop had taken Tucker's hand to help him down the steps off the porch. Tucker still remembered how big and strong his grandfather's hand felt, compared to his own. Gramma usually had Tucker in tow. He couldn't remember a time before that day when Grandpop had held on to him.

They walked through the hallway with his grandfather still holding his hand. Tucker remembered he felt like a partner in the important task of checking the church.

In the sanctuary, Grandpop told him, "We're going to pick up all bulletins and papers our friends have left in the pews. Then, we'll empty the waste baskets. Tucker, we want to leave it a better place than before we came." Tucker had remembered Grandpop's every word.

Tucker smiled as Mr. Stuart and the boys entered the building. The church was just as everyone had left it that morning. "Can you believe it. The Palm Sunday service was this morning." He shook his head in disbelief. "It feels like it was weeks ago."

"Hi, Tucker, Darren," Pastor Daily greeted. He had a large flashlight in his hand. "I have to figure out a way to get some light in the church. People have started coming in."

Tucker flashed his light down the hallway. "Where are they?"

"The few that have already arrived are down in the Fellowship Hall," the pastor said with a deep sigh. "How do you make a dark place safe for everyone?"

"I'll go down and see if I can help anyone," Mr. Stuart said as he started for the stairs. "Then, I'll go up and down the streets here, near the church, and see if people have spare blankets. I imagine the first responders will soon bring in blankets and rescue supplies."

Tucker looked down the dark hall. "Grandpop is on his way over. He said there are candles in the basement."

"That's good," the pastor said slowly. "But, candles sitting on something with an open flame could be dangerous."

"I have a solution." Joseph Moyer said as he came in with an old glass lamp with a brass base.[7] "Evening weddings here at the church used to be lit by these lamps. There are candles here in the church basement. And, if the boys will go over to our house, Rebecca will show them where they are. The candle lamps have been stored in our basement since the church was lit with electricity."

"It's a miracle," Pastor Daily steepled his fingers in praise. "Praise the Lord. Joseph, it seems like you always find a solution to our problems."

Gus jumped with excitement. "Great. We'll go. That's something we can do. I'd be happy to help." He started back out the door. "Come on guys."

"Thanks, men," Pastor Daily called after them. "All of you are a great help."

Tucker could see their backs get straighter when they heard the pastor's words. He watched as they started back down the church steps on the way back over to his house.

"Grandpop, are the candles in that large cardboard box marked, Palmer Hardware? I remember looking into that box many years ago." Tucker stopped and thought about the packages and storage containers in the basement. "Or, they could ..."

"That's right, Tucker," his grandfather answered. "Palmer Hardware. You go down there, and I'll go in and straighten the sanctuary and empty the trash baskets."

Tucker pointed his light to the clock on the wall. It was fifteen minutes before nine. "We can handle all that, Grandpop. It's ..."

His grandfather winked. "It's past my bedtime?"

Tucker blushed. "Grandpop, you get up when the rest of the world is still sleeping."

"Okay," his grandfather agreed. "I'll pick up the papers in the sanctuary and show the pastor where the paper supplies are stored. Then I'll go home. Jacob said he heard that the electricity will be back on here on this side of the highway by morning. You'll only need the candles through the night."

As Grandpop turned his attention to stray pieces of paper and other knit-pickys, Vinny, Morty, and Gus came back in. They were carrying a glass lamp in each hand.

"Great, guys," the pastor greeted with relief. His voice was beginning to sound weak and exhausted. Tucker could easily see he was tired. "I'm afraid I've forgotten where I put the last small box of matches. They could be in my pocket. After a day like this, I wouldn't know it."

"I don't have matches," Morty stammered. He dug in his pocket. In his hand was a silver lighter. He blushed. "I don't smoke, Pastor Daily. My dad gave me the lighter. It had been his when he was younger."

"Super." Pastor Daily pointed to the lamps. "You three, put a lamp in each bathroom, one on the table here in the hall, and the other three we'll take downstairs." He nodded to Tucker. "You get the candles. And, Morty, you light them. You are carrying the flame, just like the Olympic torch carrier."

Morty beamed.

"I'll go down to the basement," Tucker said as he started for the door that led down. "Then, I'll make sure that Grandpop gets home and to bed. I brought over some sandwiches. If any of the survivors are hungry, they can have them. I'll make more and bring them over."

Down in the basement, he smiled as he remembered his last expedition to the mysterious underground world of boxes and cartons. A month ago, Grandpop had sent him down for another can of Ajax cleaner. He smiled as he thought of the jingle the Colgate-Palmolive Company had printed on their box-of-six, "Stronger than dirt!"

The Palmer Hardware box was near the Ajax. That's how he had remembered its location. He reached in and started to remove six of the candles, then decided to bring the entire box upstairs.

Tucker placed the candles on the counter in the kitchen. To the three guys, he said, "Here they are. You can light up this place."

Gus was still excited to help and started upstairs for the glass lamps. "Let there be light."

When Tucker saw that Grandpop had gone home, he stayed in the kitchen. He filled the coffee maker with water and added the amount of coffee necessary to make twenty piping hot cups. With the cookie crock on the counter, he took a small plate from one of the cupboards. Arranged in a circle, a half-dozen cookies greeted the people so they would know they were welcome to help themselves. In the dim light, a young hand reached for a cookie and slipped over to one of the tables in the Fellowship Hall.

"Barry?" Tucker couldn't believe it. Ten-year-old Barry Nuemann sat at the table with his cookie. Tucker watched as the boy only nibbled small bites.

Barry looked up with vacant eyes and a dirty face. "Have they found my mom and dad, yet?"

"I don't know, Barry." Tucker pulled out a chair and sat beside him. "I just got here. I'll ask Pastor Daily." Tucker started to get up.

"No!" Barry demanded. "Don't leave me here. I don't want to be alone."

"Sure, Barry." Tucker didn't know what to say. "I'll stay with you until your parents get here." Tucker wondered how long that would be.

"Okay." The little boy said no more and bit off a large piece of the cookie.

Tucker looked around. There were two other families already enjoying Gramma's cookies. A girl, about Barry's age, smiled when Ticker looked her way. Then he had an idea. He spotted the basketball hoop that Uncle James hung on the wall for the Boy Scouts when they would meet in the church. The ball was secured in a wooden box on the floor in the corner.

"Hey, Barry, do you like basketball? How about a basketball challenge?"

Barry suddenly brightened. He wiped the crumbs from his mouth and stood up. "I'm ready. I like basketball a lot."

Tucker asked the girl in the polka dotted dress, "What's your name?"

"Linda," she said as she watched Tucker and Barry retrieve the basketball. "I like to play basketball, too."

"Okay. Now…" he thought a moment, "each shooter will have five tries at the basket. Then it's the next person's turn. We'll see who has the most baskets in …" he tried to see the clock. "I can't see it. So… let's say... who has the highest score after ten times at the basket."

Vinny, Morty, and Gus brought the candle lamps[10] downstairs. One was put on the counter of the kitchen. The other two were placed in the Fellowship Hall.

"I'd like to shoot some baskets, too," Vinney said as he squinted at the hoop.

"What do you think, Barry and Linda?" Tucker asked. "Should we let the old kids play?"

Barry dribbled the ball a few times, then said, "Well, okay. But they are taller."

"Right," Tucker agreed. "Let's make it fair." He pointed to some lines on the floor from the shuffle board court that had been painted there. "You and Linda, shoot from this free throw line. The line in a gym is fifteen feet from the backboard. So, us older kids will have to shoot from ..." He walked several yards from the hoop. "From here."

Morty strained and blinked at the hoop. "Tucker, it's too dark. We can't even see the basket from here."

"Oh, okay." Tucker thought for a minute, then remembered a stack of hymnals on top of the piano on the back wall. Even after several attempts of propping his flashlight, it continued to slip and slide. "Ah ha," he let out and hurried to the cabinet beside the piano. *There it is.* He pulled a giant roll of Scotch tape from the shelf and taped the flashlight to the songbooks. Then, it stayed, balanced between three hymnals on each side of the light by generous strips of tape. The beam pointed straight at the basketball hoop, a real homing beacon.

Each shooter took their turn, with whooping and laughing. Barry poised the ball carefully and took his best shot. It rounded in the air and slipped through the basket with no effort.

"Yeah," they hollered and clapped for joy. Tucker and the boys managed to take the children's minds off the happenings of the evening.

"Barry," a woman called out as she ran over to the boy. "You're okay." Teary eyed, she looked him over, up and down. "You're fine."

A man who Tucker figured could have been his father swooped Barry up off the floor and swung him around in a circle. "Barry, thank the Lord."

"Blankets and pillows, everybody," Darren Stuart called out as he came through the door.

"I'll bet you're tired, Barry." Tucker patted him on the back. "You can get a blanket."

"You won't have to, Honey," his mother said as tears rolled down her cheeks. She looked at other survivors as they started gathering in the room. Cupping her hand to her mouth, she whispered, "Our house is almost okay." She wrapped her arms around Barry and rocked him back and forth. "We'll just have to do some rebuilding in the kitchen. Your grandma and grandpa's house…" She looked at Tucker and Mr. Stuart as she blotted her eyes. "Their house is gone." She swallowed hard. "They're in the hospital but are doing very well. We," she stopped and hugged her son again, "we didn't know where you were. We were told that people were gathering here."

Barry hugged his mother again and pointed over his shoulder. "Tucker found things for us to do."

"God bless you, Tucker," she whispered.

"God bless Barry's grandparents. I hope they heal fast," he heard himself say. He felt stuck in a grown-up situation and hoped he was doing the right thing.

Chapter Twenty-Six
GOING HOME

The wicks in the glass lamps were turned down to dim. Tucker drug himself home as those in the church settled in for a restless sleep. Joe darted ahead and waited for him on the side porch until he got to the door. Tucker ruffled Joe's neck and scratched the silky hair behind his ears. The loyal dog quietly followed him into the house.

In the semi-dark house, Tucker sat on the first dining room chair and unlaced his muddy shoes. At first, he didn't know what to do with them. They weren't fit for the house. He stepped out on the porch and beat them across the banister, removing the larger clumps that clung to them. Back inside, he and Joe crossed the dining room and walked over to the steps. Joe seemed to know how tired Tucker was.

"That was the longest day I can remember," he whispered to Joe. Tucker's legs felt unbelievably heavy as he walked up the steps. It felt like, sometime that evening, he had changed into shoes with led-filled soles. No bouncing. No two steps at a time.

Upstairs, he slipped silently into the bathroom and quickly showered. He had to wash off the grime and tears of others from that long day. The hot water and steam soaked a little of the soreness out of his neck. He had finally slowed down enough to feel his body, and all the aches and pains he had managed to ignore when he was busy helping others. Drying off, he wrapped the towel around himself, and gathered up his dirty clothes and shoes.

The filthy clothes were held at arm's length, so he didn't get them too close. They dripped of everything from watery mud to dog poo.

Creeping quietly down the hallway, Tucker saw Tiny sleeping just outside Gramma and Grandpop's room. The little dog had to know the day was strange, a happy holiday movie that turned into a horror flick. The little dog raised her head and watched the boy and his dog as they stood at the door, then laid back down.

Tucker carefully turned the door handle to check on his grandparents. He peeked in and saw that they were both sleeping comfortably. Their breathing moved the blanket up and down, all was well.

Tucker often worried about them. They were getting old, and Tucker was aware of their slowing down. Why couldn't life just stand still, he often wondered. He wished he could choose his favorite day and stay there longer.

Joe followed Tucker into his room and lay down on the area rug. He sighed, looked at Tucker, and seemed to be satisfied that they were finally home.

Tucker flipped his jeans and shirt over the footboard of his bed. Weariness had completely taken over. He would deal with the dirty clothes in the morning. Grabbing an old sweatshirt from the floor, he pulled it over his head, slid on a pair of shorts, and fell into bed.

Images of destroyed homes and crying children flooded his mind. Everywhere his memory had recorded, there was destruction and loss. He relieved the memory of Harvey Kline's pain and winced again as if it were his own. The thought about Adam's new box of crayons. It made him smile and ache at the same time. That was all the child worried about. But there was nothing left of his house, not a single thing larger than a pencil. It had all been destroyed and blown away.

Then he remembered the basketball free throw challenge and smiled again. The kids had so much fun, and so did he and the other "big kids." In his mind's eye, he could see the ball leave his hands, arch perfectly overhead, and sink into the basket more beautifully than he had ever done before, even on the school's basketball team.

Laying there, he felt traumatized and yet entertained by the pictures behind his eyes. He also thought about his father, just a short distance down the street. Tucker had helped many people, but he hadn't checked on his own father and his dad's family. Then he thought again, and remembered how hard it was to get through the trash and demolition. And, he remembered the road block. The first responders had put up a road block just one street beyond where they helped Adam find Jacky.

He couldn't have gotten through to his father's house, and he began to feel better. That would have to be tomorrow.

Way back in the corner of his memory, he saw the picture of his mother, like the image that hung on the living room wall. She had brown curly hair and sparkling blue eyes, just like his own. What if she had needed help? What if she hadn't died?

Tucker chose not to think about sad things any more. Injured friends and neighbors were receiving medical treatment. The ones who had died were already at home in heaven. Those who were homeless were sleeping in the church, with a warm blanket over them, walls around them, and a dry roof over their head. Some had already been invited into the homes of family or friends.

As he drifted off to sleep, he knew a fact. As much as he wanted to forget the day and remember the Easter vacation that had just started a few days ago, it would be a day he would never forget.

Chapter Twenty-Seven
THE MORNING AFTER

Tucker opened his eyes the next morning as Joe quietly rested his nose on the edge of the bed. "Hi, boy," Tucker whispered, surprised by his own raspy voice. Was it from smoke that had been in the air? Or, was it complete exhaustion? He knew his body ached a little, before he even touched the floor.

The sun was shining through his bedroom window that faced the backyard. The light had reached the middle of the floor. It was like he had his own sun dial. As bright as the sun was by that hour, the day must have gotten away from him. He could tell by the light line. It had to be at least eight in the morning.

Jumping out of bed, he grabbed his Levis where they hung over the end of his bed. He looked down and frowned. Mud covered his pants up to his belt loops. More smears and clumpy dirt clustered around his pockets from jamming his hands in and out of them. He suspected his backside was also filthy from slipping and sliding through the destruction of last night. He had showered before bedtime and tried not to touch the super-grime. Then he remembered he had draped them over the foot board because he was too tired to deal with them. Shoving the dirty pants onto the floor of his closet, he pulled out an identical pair of blue jeans, minus the dirt. He had several pair of the same pants. There was no point in searching for a new look. He was perfectly satisfied with his Levi's.

The plaid shirt he chose was a favorite. It had a pattern of blue, white, and green. He knew there was a possibility he would be back out in the tornado's chaotic aftermath. But, somehow, the shirt felt comfortable. He lay on his stomach and pulled out a suitable pair of shoes. Most important, they were free from the mud and soil of the night before. With his worn but clean leather chukka boots in his hand, Tucker jumped down the steps.

Gramma looked up from the *National Geographic* with wide eyes. "Good morning. I wondered when you would get up." She motioned to the magazine. "The newspaper deliverer wasn't able to get through to Dunlap, so I'm reading about the rebuilding of London." She smiled. "You're usually an early riser. But then, you were helping long into the night. The telephone lines were put back up some time during the night." She placed the magazine on the table beside her. "The pastor called and told me all of the things you did to help friends last evening. You were really a good worker."

"Thanks, Gramma." Tucker headed to the coat rack. "I'm going to go over to the church."

"Eat some breakfast first, Tucker." She started for the kitchen. "Volunteers are trying to feed the survivors sheltering in the Fellowship Hall. I don't know how much food they have collected over there yet."

"Right," Tucker agreed, pulling a medium size mixing bowl from the cupboard. "I'll eat some Wheaties before I go over. I want to see how everyone is doing." He dumped the other half of the cereal box into the bowl and pored milk over the flakes. Tucker ate the Wheaties fast enough he couldn't even taste the mild, toasted grains, with the slight hint of honey and sugar.

Gramma patted Tucker on the chest. "That should tide you over for a little while."

He chose one of Gramma's soup spoons to shovel his breakfast in faster. Slurping it down by the mouth full, he tried to ask, "Have you heard if anyone we know was hurt yesterday, besides Harvey Kline?"

Grandpop came in and slowly poured another cup of coffee. "The electricity is back on. They said on the radio that the Midway Trailer Park was leveled. A newscaster on WTRC said, even though the paper was not delivered to the Dunlap area today, Paul Huffman from the newspaper had written that at least one-hundred mobile homes were destroyed. Huffman said the trailers were ripped off their foundations, spun around in the air, then dropped, crashing to the ground. Many people were killed." Grandpop sipped from his cup. "We don't know any of their names yet or how many survived."

"What about Sunnyside?" Tucker asked as he washed and dried the bowl.

Grandpop shook his head. "It's flattened."

"And my dad?" Tucker removed his coat from the hook at the door and stared at the floor. "Have you heard anything?"

His grandfather patted his shoulder. "I haven't heard anything about Sean yet. You know your dad. If the house was blown away, he would have found a way to save everyone."

Tucker was determined. "I'm going over to the church to see for myself if he and his wife and Matty are among the survivors." Shaking his head, he thought about his little brother, just a baby. "Matty is really little."

Grandpop drank more Folgers. "Don't you worry about Sean. We would have probably heard if they were injured. I'll be right over. Someone at the church might need something."

Chapter Twenty-Eight
LIFE NEEDS REASSURANCE SOMETIMES

When Tucker entered the church, Mrs. Hunter hurried up with a copy of the *Elkhart Truth*. "Look, Tucker. My husband was able to get into town to get today's newspaper. It's on the front page." She handed him the first section of the paper.

"What's on the front page?" Tucker asked as he opened it to page one. There, spread across the paper, was a photograph of the double headed tornado that hit the Midway Trailer Park[11]. "Oh my goodness," he gasped. "That's what I saw."

"Good, Tucker, you're here," Pastor Daily's shoulders squared a little as Tucker came into the church. "We have a lot to do."

"Okay," Tucker agreed with a blank expression. "Like ... what?"

"I got a telephone call after the lines were back up last night," the pastor began, almost giddy. Tucker had never seen him like that before. "The call came in about 2 a.m. I was finally sleeping deeply." He frantically ran his fingers through his hair while pacing back and forth.

"Tucker, I didn't know who it was." He threw his hand to his mouth to cover a gasp. "The person on the other end of the line said, 'Good evening. This is the President.' I thought it was someone just harassing me after the day I had. I told you. I didn't know who it was. I just snapped back, 'Sure it is, fella,' and hung up on him." Daily tormented his innocent hair again. "The phone rang again, and the same guy said, 'Pastor Daily, I'll give you the switchboard's phone number for the White House. Call the operator and they'll connect us so we can talk.' I was shocked." Pastor Daily shook his head. "A calm, quiet voice hummed into the receiver, 'The White House.' I couldn't believe it, Tucker," he chattered on at full speed, nearly short of breath. "I said, 'This is Pastor Phillip Daily. I am supposed to call the President.'"

"Yes, Sir," the switchboard operator responded. "He is expecting your call."

The Pastor rattled on, pacing back and forth. "Tucker, the President of the United States was expecting my telephone call. The President himself."

"I never heard of anything like that," Tucker flustered. He couldn't think of any reason for the head of the free world to call Dunlap. "The President? What did he want?"

"That's just it. He said he had been told about the devastation here in Dunlap. He said that other counties in Indiana were hit, too, but Dunlap got the worst of it. He wanted me to know, that he's coming here later this morning."

Tucker nearly staggered backward. "Here? The President is coming here? To Dunlap?"

"That's what the man said." The pastor swallowed hard. "Sheriff Springer also called this morning." He repeated, rubbing his forehead. "He said he was contacted about the President's visit and said the leader of the free world will be here at 11 a.m." Pastor Daily checked his wrist watch with trembling hands. "He'll be here in about two hours."

"What do you want me to do?" Tucker asked as he hung his coat in the open closet area. His insides began to rattle around. He was beginning to feel that the pastor's anxious mood was contagious. What on earth could Tucker McBride do to get ready for a visit from the President? "Grandpop is coming over to see if you need anything."

"Great." Pastor Daily sighed. "I can always depend on Joseph."

Tucker started for the steps. "I'm going to see if I can find someone." Before he got to the stairs, he added, "Let me know what I can do. I'll be downstairs, looking for … someone." At the bottom of the steps, he pushed open the double doors that led into the Fellowship Hall.

Many more families than the night before were sitting together at the tables, eating doughnuts. An open box revealed they were donated by Hudson's Bakery. At another table, a mother was rubbing a small child's back as he lay his head on the table. A couple Tucker recognized from his old paper route were silently sitting together, their eyes like glazed glass. Six-year-old Gracie Gorman walked up carefully and handed the woman her teddy bear. He watched as the woman took it and was able to force a smile. She rubbed the fuzzy cloth of the stuffed animal and seemed to relax a little, as her shoulder settled in comfort.

Tucker pushed on the swinging door to the kitchen and stepped inside. Maybe his dad was in there. But there was only a woman standing near the refrigerator. Mrs. Hunter, from the school, was lining up five loaves of bread on the counter and putting two gallons of milk in the Frigidaire. "Hi, Tucker."

Tucker knew that Mrs. Hunter didn't live in Sunnyside nor in a trailer at Midway. "Was your home affected, too, Mrs. Hunter?" he asked. "Or, do you know someone here?"

"Sure," she said as she slowly closed the refrigerator door. "Many of the young adults have been my students over the years. Some of the survivors are my students now."

Tucker didn't know what to say. He knew how much she cared for those who were in her classes. "I'm sorry, Mrs. Hunter." Then he thought, "If they are in your class now, do I know them?"

She smiled and nodded. "Kevin Reilly, and his little sister and parents are in there." She pointed to the Fellowship Hall. "Patty Schmidt and her family are here. I'm thankful each of them survived the twister that destroyed their entire homes. They can always rebuild."

"Kevin and Patty are here? They hadn't arrived before I left last night." He shook his head in disbelief. "I didn't know."

"They're fine," Mrs. Hunter assured him. "They aren't hurt, just rattled about losing their school books, their clothes, their band instruments, and everything they own."

"What do I say to them?" Tucker had no idea how to sooth their losses.

"It sounds like you did a wonderful job last evening," she assured him.

As he turned, he bumped into Christy Tree. "Christy!" he gasped. "Is your family okay?"

"Yes, yes, Tucker. I came over to see if there were any small children here." She lifted the sack she was carrying. "I brought some children's books Mom had saved in a box in the attic. I thought I'd read to the kids. I just finish reading one of the books to them. They laughed and seemed to forget about the wind for a little while."

Suddenly, Tucker started to relive the darkness of the night before and began to feel the effect of the tornadoes. He relived seeing Mosher's barn spin in the air in the vivid pictures in his mind. He closed his eyes and shook off the dreaded experience. Then, he thought again about his father. "Have you ... seen my dad and Matthew? Little Matty is only a few months old."

"No ...," Christy said thoughtfully.

Mrs. Hunter overheard the conversation. "Sean McBride? Your dad?"

Tucker's mouth opened. "I didn't know you knew him."

"Of course I do," she said, smiling. "I go into his little grocery store often. In fact, this morning, I saw one of the first responders securing lines over in Sunnyside. He told me the tornado skipped over your dad's house and store and took out everything across the street from him."

Tucker gave a releasing exhale. He was worried but wanted to sound like an adult, in charge of his feelings. "Tornadoes do the craziest things."

Chapter Twenty-Nine
WHERE'S MICKY?

"Tucker." Freddie came hurrying in, his hands shaking anxiously. He looked around frantically at the clusters of people who had taken refuge in the church. "Have you seen Micky?"

"Micky?" Tucker asked as he glanced around the Fellowship Hall. "No. Do you mean he's missing?"

Freddie's head hung and shook negatively. "We can't find him anywhere. Mom and Dad have searched every inch of the house and yard, up and down the street. When they went out to check the yard, Mom said the door was unlocked. She was pacing around the living room in desperation." In his hand he carried a stocking cap. "If he's outside, he forgot his hat."

Christy's expression changed and energy overtook her. "What about the tepee? Micky was so proud that he had helped put it up. Maybe he went back there."

"You are brilliant!" Freddie shouted and headed toward the door. "That has to be it." He darted up the steps. "At least, I hope that's where he is."

"I'll help you," Tucker offered as he caught up and locked step with him.

Christy laid the sack of books on the kitchen counter, skipped a little, and was right behind them. "It was my idea. I'm coming, too."

At the church door, Goldie Washington and her son, Johnny, were just coming in. "Tucker," Goldie gasped. "I am so glad to see that you're alright. How about your grandparents? Are they okay? I saw that the house is still standing."

"Hi, Mrs. Washington. Yes, they are fine," Tucker assured her.

She burst with excitement. "They said on the radio that the survivors were gathering here in the church. I came right out. I had to see for myself that Rebecca and Joseph were alright. When our choir from the A.M.E. church in Elkhart comes out to sing for your church, your grandmother has been wonderful." Goldie blotted a tear that rolled down her cheek. "She has become my close friend." Clearing her throat, she added, "I had to come out to see that she was safe and that your home was spared."

Tucker smiled and looked at Freddie who stood waiting to go over to the Moyer house. "You are welcome to come over, Mrs. Washington. Johnny, you can come with us if it's okay with your mom. Freddie's cousin is lost. Micky is only five."

"Oh, my goodness," Mrs. Washington gasped. "A sweet little boy like that. He's five-years-old? Yes, Johnny, see if you can help find him."

"Hi, Johnny." Christy greeted. "It's good to see you again."

"It's good to see you, too." To Tucker, he added, "Great, Tucker. We'll find him." Johnny brightened as he followed Tucker and Christy outside. Even though he attended school in Elkhart, and played on an opposing basketball team, he and Tucker were friends. A couple of times a year, his mother's choir shared the rhythms and enthusiasm of their African American music with the friends at Tucker's church.

At Tucker's house, all five of them went inside. Gramma had just finished washing the breakfast dishes and was "patting" the kitchen, wiping down the counter and refrigerator. The room had the slight herbal smell of Ivory Snow Flakes that she had washed the dishes in.

Gramma looked up from her cleaning. "Goldie Washington, as I live and breathe."

"I had to come out and make sure you were all okay," Goldie said as she gave Gramma a big hug.

"You were lucky you came out early this morning," Gramma said as she guided her friend into the living room. "The President will be here this morning. I wouldn't be surprised if they close the roads."

"The President? Of the United States of America?" Goldie gasped.

Uncle Jacob came in from the kitchen. "They might enforce Marshall Law." He looked out the window. "There could be a lot of looters, trying to take advantage of the fact that many people are out of their homes. Even those houses that were destroyed, could have valuables buried under the rubble."

"Oh, my," Goldie exclaimed. "That's awful."

"Mom." Johnny jumped in before his mom and her friend could dive deeper into a lengthy conversation. "I'm going with Tucker to look for Micky."

"Yes, sweetheart. You go find that dear little boy," she said and patted Johnny on the back.

With all of them ready to search for Micky, Tucker said, "Let's go."

Chapter Thirty
JOE HELPED

Tucker led the way through the kitchen, down the few steps to the summer house, and out the back door. But it was Freddie who quickly took the lead.

"Micky!" Freddie yelled. He ran around the corner of the house, through the backyard, and out across the alley. In a flash, he darted into the tepee. His shoulders slumped and his smile faded, along with his hope of finding the little guy. The tepee was empty.

"Okay, okay," Tucker said with his fist pounding his hand. "He isn't here. Let's wait a minute and think."

Johnny looked inside the Native American dwelling with wide eyes. "Tucker, where on earth did this come from?"

"It belongs to Gramma's cousin, Sam Treadway," Tucker said slowly, as he too looked into the tepee. As much as they all wanted to find Micky in the dwelling, there was no one there. "Sam had stored the tepee in our attic and told me I could put it up if I wanted to. We all worked on it on Friday after school. Even Micky helped."

"Micky," Freddie whispered. "Where is he?"

"Let's sit down for a powwow," Christy suggested as she sat on the ground in cross-legged style. "It doesn't seem like he would have gone far."

"Okay," Tucker began as they sat in the circle. He asked Freddie, "Do you know if Micky slept in the house last night? When was the last time anyone saw him?"

Freddie pounded his index finger in the grass. "Mom tucked him in after the tornado passed. We all assumed it was safe."

Christy touched his shoulder gently. "It was safe, Freddie. The tornadoes passed, and it was all over in no time."

"I know, but …" He studied each blade of grass beneath him. Unable to look at anyone, he stared at the ground.

Tucker thought about being only five-years-old and seeing a tornado coming straight at him. "Was he afraid?"

"Yeah," Freddie said and cleared his throat. "He was crying even after the tornado passed. I heard him sniffling when I passed the guest room door."

"Did he talk to anyone after he went to bed?" Johnny asked. "To you or to your mom?"

Freddie shrugged. "Mom tucked him in."

"But," Tucker began slowly, trying not to sound like he was interrogating him. "Close your eyes and see what happened last evening. Did you guys go to the basement?"

Freddie kept his eyes shut as he tried to relive what was so hard to experience the first time and just as hard in his memory. "Yeah, we all went to the basement. Micky didn't want to. He said that we wouldn't be able to see the tornado from down there. Dad told him it would be okay. He said that someone would probably take a picture of it."

Tucker waited for Freddie to stop talking before asking, "Did Micky say anything about that?"

Freddie kept his eyes closed. "Yes. He said, that wasn't what bothered him. He wanted to be able to see it so he could run away from it. He said he had to be up higher to know what was going on. The tornado was in the sky."

Christy smiled. "So, the little guy didn't want to be caught off guard, unable to see what was coming his way."

"Right," Freddie agreed, then frowned as he remembered something else. "He said that his house was made of bricks. He kept asking if the wood on our house would break apart if a tornado hit it. Dad couldn't answer him." Freddie looked intently at Tucker. "Dad didn't want to lie to him."

"Sure," Tucker agreed so Freddie would feel better. "I understand." Then his face lit up, and he smiled. "I have an idea." He jumped up and took the cap from Freddie's hand. "Joe," he called to his dog, laying outside the tepee entrance. Tucker lowered the hat to Joe's nose. "Find Micky, Joe."

Joe sniffed the cap and started running toward the side street with Tucker close behind.

"Wait!" Freddie shouted as he followed. "Where are you going?"

"We're with you," Christy said as she caught up to Tucker, with Johnny beside her.

Tucker crossed the road again and turned, running backward. "The church was designated as the shelter for the area soon after the tornado blew through. So, it was unlocked all night so people could get in. I left pretty late. I know that the building was still open then."

"Yeah," Freddie agreed.

Tucker laughed as he jerked the door open. "Follow us." In the rare, emergency situation, Joe was permitted inside the church. He darted in cautiously and sat, waiting obediently, halfway down the hall.

Christy stopped when she went into the church. She saw Tucker slowdown in the middle of the hall. Gasping with a knowing smile, she whispered, "The tower. He thought the tower was leaning, leaning into the wind."

Tucker stopped at the narrow tower door. Silently, he said a prayer, asking God to help him find Micky, and to help him to remember to be quiet while looking for him. With his hand on the door knob, he twisted. It opened.

"Micky knew the tepee was stronger if it leaned into the wind. Maybe he thought the tower would be strong because he thought it leans into the wind."

They all scrambled up the winding steps to the bell tower like troops in cotton combat boots. At the top of the stairs, they stopped for Tucker to push the trap door open and ease into the tower-like space above. It was an open-air steeple with tar paper covering the floor, sealing it off from any rain damage.

Tucker looked around as the wind blew on his face. "Micky would be able to see another tornado coming from here. It couldn't sneak up on him."

The clear blue sky overhead was peaceful now, and the sun smiled on the Dunlap corner. Tucker was right. He found Micky calmly sleeping on the tower floor. Before they woke him up, Tucker put his finger to his lips and pointed to where Sunnyside had been the previous morning. If Micky had gotten to the top of the brick church while it was still dark, he may not have been able to see what had happened to the neighborhood just north of the corner.

Tucker had been out in the chaos and the grief of the Tornado for hours. He helped in the rain, and the dark, but he hadn't been able to see it all either, even after the stars came out. As he stood there in the top of the tower, far above the street, his heart hurt for all his friends who lived in Sunnyside.

This was also Christy and Johnny's first sight of what was left of the subdivision. Johnny was stunned and said nothing. Christy only mouthed a shocked, "Crackers."

Freddie glanced north briefly, shook his head, and stooped down beside Micky. "Hey there, Micky. Are you hungry? Breakfast has been waiting for you."

A gentle breeze blew through the top of the church, like a whisper of hope. Tucker knew they had to awaken the boy, but wished they could carry him down asleep and away from the bird's eye view.

Micky woke up, leaned on his elbow, and started to get up. Quickly, Tucker tapped him on the shoulder, turning him away from the sight no one wanted him to see.

"Hey, Micky," Tucker began, hoping to find out how long he had been up there. "Weren't you cold last night? When did you climb up here?"

"I don't know," Micky said as he yawned.

Christy approached it from a different angle. "Was everybody asleep when you left Freddie's house?" she asked, hoping to help with a positive tone. No one wanted him to feel like he was being scolded.

Micky tried to remember the events of early that morning. "I woke up in my bed at Freddie's house and looked out the window. I tried to see if the tornado was coming back." He stood up with Christy's help as she spun him away from the northern view. "I could see that there was a little light in the church, and I remembered the tower. I thought I could see everything from way up here."

"The lights didn't come back on until about 5 a.m.," Tucker reminded them. "It would still have been dark at that time."

Freddie put his arm around Micky's shoulders. "You can see all around up here," he agreed and pointed to the south, to the Cooper house. "See, right there is my house." He pointed again. "And that's where Christy and her family live." When Micky tried to turn around, Freddie added, "We'd better go."

Tucker thought of another reason to make him feel good about abandoning his safe nest. "Oh, and Micky, finish your breakfast in time and maybe you can see the President. He's coming to show everyone his support."

"The President of the United States of America?" Micky asked with a gasp.

Tucker laughed. "The President of these United States of America."

Christy motioned for Johnny to stand with her behind Micky. Even if Micky turned around, he would only see blue jeans. Freddie led the way down the steps, assisting Micky the whole way. Tucker was the last one. As the others went down a few steps, he lowered the trap door overhead. When he got to the hall, his grandfather was there.

"Joe told me where you were," he said as he rubbed the top of the dog's head. "When she got down from the tower, Christy told me about Freddie's cousin," Grandpop said, shaking his head in amazement. "I just saw Freddie go out the door to take the boy home. He said to thank you very much. He'll talk to you later. I told him he's welcome on the porch when the President drives past." He gripped Tucker's shoulder. "Christy also said, you figured out where Micky might be." He looked at his grandson lovingly. "I am so proud of you. I'll lock this tower door. Don't go away." He started to put the key in the lock, then said, "Your mother would be proud of you, too."

Tucker smiled at his grandfather and friends. The best part was what Grandpop said about his mother. She would have been proud of him.

Chapter Thirty-One
A SHORT STOP

After Freddie left, and Christy went home to tell her mom where she was and what happened to Micky Cooper, Grandpop took Tucker by the sleeve. "After the tornadoes hit, the storm continued, and the wind blew for hours, knocking out the phone lines."

Tucker was confused. "But Pastor Daily said the President called him last night."

"He did," Grandpop said as he pointed and directed Tucker and Johnny to the door. "The telephones went out soon after the tornado went through. They were back on by 2 p.m." He opened the door and kept talking as he walked down the steps. "Your Uncle Jerry said he also got real busy on his ham radio during the night, with people checking on loved ones." At the foot of the steps, he stopped. "Tucker, Uncle Jerry came down while you were over here. He said, your half-brother, Bobby, was able to get a ham radio buff there in California to send a message to Jerry. Bobby wanted to make sure you and all your friends were okay ... and your dad and Matthew, Matty as your dad calls him. You can't call your dad. The lines in Sunnyside are all still laying in all the broken homes. You'll have to go down to his house."

"Mrs. Hunter was down in the kitchen. She said she heard that Dad's house and the grocery were spared." Tucker dug his toe in the gravel at the edge of the road. "I probably should go down and see if they need anything. I'll drive my Model A." He looked at Johnny. "Do you want to ride in my car."

Johnny shook his head in disbelief. "Tucker, I've ridden with you in your car before. And, you still don't have a driver's license."

"Of course not." Tucker rolled his eyes. "I'm not old enough to have a driver's license. But you'll have to admit, I'm careful."

"You might have to be more careful than usual, Tucker," Grandpop warned as they crossed the side street. "Jerry said he's been using his short-wave to keep up on the news and any information about Dunlap since the tornado hit. He said the whole area is temporarily under martial law. That means, with the number of people in emergency situations, and so much destruction, the President has imposed military rule over our little area. That replaces civilian authorities. People won't even be able to drive into Dunlap for a little while.

"Tucker, some sergeant might not like that you drive without license. So, be careful." He started up the side steps. "Before you go, we are nearly out of coffee. I need for you to run over to Winkler's. And, here's thirty cents. That'll be enough for a pound of Folgers coffee. Keep the three cents change."

"Okay, Grandpop," Tucker said as he and Johnny headed over to the grocery.

Crossing the highway out front had become quite a challenge. Even though there were fewer cars from Elkhart and Goshen coming into the area to check on family and friends, there were many more military vehicles on the road. Their camouflage pattern could be seen everywhere.

"Hi, Mr. Winkler," Tucker announced as he walked through the door. "Is everything okay over here? This is my friend, Johnny Washington."

"Hi, young man," Mr. Winkler greeted. "Yeah, Tucker, we're all okay. The house is fine. Our neighbor, Judy and Dave's house was damaged a lot. They're staying at our house for a few days. Judy's mom and dad's condo in Florida will be available on Friday. They are going down there and relax for a month or two while their house is being repaired. Since her mom and dad will be up here, they'll oversee Judy's rebuild. My wife is still shaken up a little."

"Hope she's okay soon," Tucker offered as he walked over to the shelf of coffee, tea, and Carnation instant hot chocolate mix. He selected a can of Folgers and started for the cash register. "Wow, time in Florida. How can he be away from work?"

"He's a writer. He can write anywhere."

Tucker looked up, excitedly. "A writer? I've never met a writer before."

"Sure you have." Mr. Winkler took the thirty cents Tucker had placed on the counter. "He was on your paper route. Horris Mannigan. He writes the Barnwood Boys Mysteries."

Johnny jumped in. "I love those books."

Tucker added, "I read a few. Wow, I didn't know that I knew the author." He wondered how many people in his neighborhood that he thought he knew, he may not have known at all. He shook his head.

Winkler made the change. "You be careful if you have to go anywhere."

Tucker smiled. "I will. I want to be back from my errand quickly. The President will be here around 11 a.m."

The grocer blinked with an absent stare. "The president of what?"

"Of all of us," Tucker said with a laugh. He hurried out the door and crossed the street.

Chapter Thirty-Two
CHECKING ON THE FAMILY

Tucker hurried through the house, dropped off the coffee, and he and Johnny headed toward his 1931 Ford. He had driven freely all over Dunlap and to counties beyond Elkhart with no problem. Would it be different today? Would he be stopped?

Outside, the backyard was scattered with pieces of roofing shingles, scraps of paper Tucker didn't recognize, but nowhere did Tucker see one seed of grass. He smiled to himself, and mumbled, "I told Uncle Jacob."

Johnny looked around. "You told him what?"

"He had me help him sow grass seed on Saturday," Tucker explained as he opened the garden gate. "I told him the radio was reporting the possibility of wind and rain. With no electricity, we didn't really know what was going on. It's back on, but I haven't heard anything this morning. I haven't been home."

Tucker smiled. Every time he looked at his old Model A Ford, he smiled. The inside may have had that stale antique smell that horsehair stuffed seats have and a style to match, but it was his. Tucker solved the strange sweet and dusty odor of the horsehair by sticking a little sack of potpourri under his seat. He bought the potpourri, made of dried roses and lavender, cinnamon sticks, cloves, dried orange slices, and decorated with pine cones at Winkler's.

They hopped into the car, and Tucker pulled out of the driveway into the alley, around onto Harvest Avenue, then left on Moyer Avenue, and stopped at the highway. With no traffic light, a man in a standard Army fatigue uniform of olive drab directed traffic. He was checking every car that went from Elkhart to Goshen and back. The corporal waved Tucker passed, across traffic.

"Maybe they are just checking people who are traveling between cities and beyond," Johnny suggested. "Not within Dunlap."

"I hope you're right," Tucker whispered, as if the corporal could hear him inside the car with the windows rolled up.

It seemed to Tucker that Johnny couldn't look at all the destruction as he kept his eyes on his fingernails. He rubbed his forehead, blocking his vision as he rubbed.

It was only a mile down to Sean's house. Yet, it always seemed like his dad was in another state, or maybe a different state of mind. Since Tucker had never lived with his father, his "family" lived in Gramma and Grandpop's house.

Tucker drove slowly. Not because he was afraid he'd be stopped by the US Military. But, because he had to see the area around him. Now the light of day was shining on the entire community on his right, where it was flattened and gone. What the tornado may have left behind in the middle of the road is every nail that had held those homes together.

"My goodness." Johnny breathed out slowly. "I had no idea what it would look like. Many houses are damaged but many more are just ... gone."

Tucker pulled his car into the gravel driveway beside his dad's house. He hoped the sound of the stones under his tires was not the sound of nails or glass. "The roof looks okay." Checking the rest of the house through the windshield of his car, he realized he was stalling.

Johnny studied the one story, modest house. "The windows on this side of the house aren't broken. That's good."

Tucker took a deep breath, put his hand on the car's door handle, and mumbled dryly, "Well, come on."

"You don't sound very enthusiastic," Johnny pointed out.

"I am, sorta." He closed the car door. "I'll just say, my dad and I haven't been real close."

"That's too bad," Johnny said quietly. "I wish my dad had made it home from the war."

"Johnny," Tucker put his arm around his friend's shoulder, "you are right. I should thank God that Sean is still alive." At the door, he knocked three times and turned the doorknob. "Hello," he hollered into the empty kitchen.

"Tucker?" Sean called from the dark living room. "Come in."

"Hi," Tucker greeted, then got to the reason he had come. "With the electricity and telephones still out over here in the storm riddled area, Bobby got a ham radio operator to message Uncle Jerry to check on everyone. Bobby was worried. I came down to see if everyone is okay."

"Yes, we're fine. No damage here." His dad stopped as his eyes looked down. "You mean Bobby wanted to know how we were, too?"

"Sure, Dad," Tucker answered, then realized how often he avoided calling Sean, Dad.

"But, across the street, oh my," Sean continued. At that moment, his wife brought the baby into the kitchen.

"I thought you might want to see Matty," she said.

"Matty?" Johnny asked.

Tucker smiled at the six-month-old baby. "This is Matthew, they call him Matty, my baby brother. Matty, this is my friend, Johnny Washington."

Matty reached out his small hand to Tucker and leaned toward him with outstretched arms. His bright face was covered with happiness.

"Hi, Matty." Tucker melted by the baby's warm smile. He reached out and took Matty in his arms. "Wow," he said bouncing him a little, "you're a big boy."

Matty reached for Tucker's nose and grabbed ahold of it.

"Ouch." Tucker laughed. Then he teased Matty by touching the end of his little nose.

"Here," Matty's mom reached for him. "I'll take him."

Tucker kissed Matty's cheek and handed him back to his mother. "Bobby was concerned, so I came down." He started to turn to leave, then stopped. "Grandpop said that Simon Winkler was open most of the night and is still open, or open again. We needed coffee, and I went over. I noticed he was out of bread. Probably because the church is where the people who survived the tornado are staying. Since we are under martial law right now, I don't think we'd be able to get into town. Do you have any bread left at your store?"

"Martial law?" Sean gasped. "I hadn't heard that. But then, I haven't tried to go anywhere." His jacket was hanging on the back of one of the kitchen chairs. Picking it up, he said, "Yes, sure, I still have bread at the store."

Tucker and Johnny followed Sean next door and into the small store that helped community friends pick up milk and bread, coffee and other small items they may have forgotten in town.

Sean removed a red can of Folgers coffee. "Here, maybe the church could use some. No charge."

Tucker was surprised. Still he had seen his dad's generosity a few other times.

"The bread is here." He pointed to a shelf of bread, doughnuts, and other pastries. "It's twelve cents a loaf. But if you think the church could use it, I'll sell it, five loaves for forty cents, not sixty."

"That sounds great," Johnny said as he slapped Tucker on the back.

Tucker agreed. "Sounds good to me, too."

His dad removed a rather large, tan paper sack from under the counter and put the can of coffee and loaves of bread inside. Entering the sale and Tucker's fifty cent piece into the cash register, he removed a dime from the cash drawer and handed the sack and change to Tucker.

"I also believe that you like potato chips." He dropped an airtight wax paper bag of New Era Potato Chips in the sack. From the candy display on the counter, he added several Baby Ruth candy bars, three Clark Bars, and half a dozen Hershey's Milk Chocolate candy bars to the sack. "The chips and candy are on the house, Tucker."

"Thanks, the President is coming today to see what the government can do to help. We're all going to sit on the porch and watch the goings-on." Tucker picked up the sack. "We'll make a candy party out of it."

"That sounds good," his father said with a chuckle. "Now you be careful driving back. If the military is guarding the neighborhood, they might not take to a fourteen-year-old driving a car."

"Thanks, Dad," Tucker said, thankful that there had been a moment when his dad acted like a dad.

Chapter Thirty-Three
WHO IS COMING?

The main corner in Dunlap, where Butch's service station and Winkler's Grocery sat across the highway from the Moyer's house and the church, was the center of everyone's attention. That morning, it seemed like all of Dunlap from miles around had gathered on that one pinpointed spot. Friends from way over where the bridge spanned the Elkhart River were lined up along US 33, as well as the aunts, uncles, cousins, and neighbors who lived in the neighborhood. Everyone who could get to that one crossroad in northern Indiana was there.

Many from the city who had driven out before the roads were closed lined the sides of the street, waiting for the President to pass by. They didn't care what political party he represented. They only cared that he came to little Dunlap, Indiana, to say he cared about their loss. Grandpop, Gramma, Tucker, and Betsy sat on the swing and chairs on their front porch to take in all the fuss. Goldie and Johnny Washington stayed at the Moyers' to get a look at the President. Tucker was amazed. He talked out loud to himself. "The President will drive by our house." It was something he almost couldn't believe.

"Hi, guys," Freddie, Micky, and Christy all greeted as they came around the corner. The boys were in their usual school clothing. But Christy had on a pair of navy blue, seersucker slacks her mother had bought for her the week before.

Christy explained, "If you can't dress a little nicer for the President, then who?" She walked up the front steps, threw her leg over the porch banister, and sat on it like she was riding a horse. "Micky, come here. You can ride the same pony I'm riding to see the President."

Freddie sat down on the top step. "The Moyers have the best spot in the area."

Johnny sat beside him, excited. He kept stretching to see down the street, anxious to see the President.

"Hi, Freddie," Gramma greeted. "How is your mother today, having a young one around and all?"

"She and Dad are going to walk up here in just a minute," Freddie said as he nodded at Micky. "She said she just wanted to enjoy the quiet for a while."

"I understand," Gramma said with a little laugh. She brushed some blowing hair from her forehead and tried to tighten the bun in the back of her hair.

"Here, Rebecca, let me help you," Goldie offered. She got out of the porch chair and came around behind the swing. With a few easy twists, tucks, and replacement of the hair pins, Goldie had Gramma's hair in place just as finely as a hairdresser in a fancy salon would have done.

Gramma patted her hair with her fingertips. "Goldie, this is great. Thank you."

Grandpop watched the gathering group and smiled. "Micky, see that low hanging branch in the tree right there?"

Micky nodded. "The one that looks like a swing seat?"

"Yep," Grandpop said and pointed. "Tucker can help you shinny up the trunk so you can sit up there. You'd be able to see real good. Just don't start getting down until Tucker helps you."

"Thanks, Mr. Moyer," Micky bubbled as he dismounted the porch rail.

Standing at the base of the walnut tree, he waited as Tucker laced his fingers together creating a small elevator. Micky stepped on the hands, and Tucker slowly raised him the several feet to the outstretched limb. "Shucks, I can see everything from here," Micky beamed.

A few minutes later, Freddie's parents came up to the corner and stopped. "Micky!" Viola Cooper shouted, her hand gripped her chest.

"He's alright, Viola," Gramma assured her. "It's the best view on the corner. Do you and Harlin want to come up here on the porch. We can squeeze you in."

"There's room here on the steps, Mom," Freddie offered and scooted over.

Viola shrugged. "Thanks, Rebecca. But I think we'll just stay here." She put her hand to her ear and listened to the chattering all around her. "It's nice and quiet over here." Then she added, "You sit still up there, Micky. Freddie will help you when you want to get down."

"He'll be fine," Uncle Jacob assured her. "He's like Zacchaeus in the book of Luke. Jesus was going through Jericho and, since Zaccheus was short, he climbed a sycamore tree so he could hear better. I'm not saying that the President and Jesus had equal missions. I'm just talking about how a short guy solved his problem."

"Then stay, Micky," Viola said as she laughed. "Just don't jump down."

Suddenly, Sheriff Springer's black and white Ford sedan led the way down South Main Street, with the car's emergency, "gumball" light rotating on the car's roof, and the siren blaring. The President's limousine was next in the procession, followed by Deputy Fletcher's squad car.

When the limo slowed to a stop right in front of the Moyer's house, the side window slowly lowered and a hand appeared. It waved to all those gathered there. The whole procession was like a small circus had rolled into town. A person in the back seat of the limo leaned forward and pointed. Through the open window, Tucker could see that it was the President of the United States, pointing at Micky.

"Mr. President, I presume," the President called out to Micky.

Micky giggled and wiggled so much he nearly fell out of the tree. The President had noticed him.

The Dunlap corner, with all the friends and strangers who had gathered, buzzed with excitement. Even a reporter from the *Elkhart Truth* took pictures not more than a few yards from the cozy balcony on a porch. Several views were pointed right at Tucker's house. One appeared to be focused on Micky up in the tree. Later, the pictures would all be part of a multi-page spread in the evening newspaper.

Micky was excited. He swung his feet vigorously and smiled widely.

When the three-car caravan turned left at the corner, Tucker was confused. "Where are they going? The shelter is at the church." He jumped off the banister and hurried down the steps, following the President's car. "I bet they're going to the fire station."

"Tucker, no," Gramma called after him. "I don't think the military will let you get near him."

"It'll be okay, Gramma," Tucker assured her as he kept walking. "Don't forget, my cousin is the Fire Chief."

Gramma laughed and called after him. "I won't forget, Tucker. Don't you forget, the Chief is my grandson, ya know."

Tucker trotted down the sidewalk, dodging people who had gathered along the road and in their yard. When he crossed the street, he could see he was right. The Sherrif's car and limousine had stopped at the department in the next block.

Already, a crowd had gathered at the Volunteer Fire Station. Tucker watched for an opening to squeeze through and casually followed everyone into the building, just like he was supposed to be there. Inside the station, all the department volunteers gathered to greet the man they would soon escort through the rubble of former homes. Tucker had slipped inside and stood off in the back, just to see the historical event. His cousin, Clive, shook the President's hand. Tucker beamed with pride. Many were his family.

Another cousin, Valerie, stood behind a table and served a cup of coffee to the head of the entire country. Tucker could see the hot steam rising from the cup. He muffled a laugh as nervous Valerie accidently spilled coffee on the President's pinstriped suit. The President took his handkerchief from his pocked and brushed at the wet spot.

Clive Moyer didn't notice the spill before he stepped closer to give a report of the events of the day before. "Mr. President, I welcome you to the Dunlap Volunteer Fire Department. After you have enjoyed some coffee and met some of the folks, I'll show you around the area. We lost many friends yesterday. I'm sure you will encounter a lot of people still experiencing profound grief. The tornadoes killed forty-five here in Dunlap and injured many more. Thirty-three of those who died were friends who lived in the Midway Trailer Court which was flattened. There was a double-headed twister at Midway. Many additional homes were destroyed by the second tornado in the Sunnyside subdivision. I have to caution you. It may be hard to walk in any of the areas hit by the tornadoes. You'll have to be real careful, Mr. President."

"Thank you, Mr. Moyer," the President offered his hand. "I will be careful, but I want to see for myself. Let me assure you, the government will help." He took the paper napkin Valerie handed him and tried to soak up some of the coffee from his white shirt and suit lapels.

Tucker had a little trouble swallowing the lump in his throat. He hadn't thought much about the President before. The family listened to the news every evening, but that was more like listening to *Lux Presents Hollywood,* a radio dramatization of distant events. He hadn't really thought that the President and other government officials were real people, in real jobs, doing real work. Yet, there he was, Mr. President.

Chapter Thirty-Four
COME FLY WITH ME

After the President toured the devastated areas of Sunnyside and the trailer park, Tucker followed him back to the church. Christy and Freddie were still sitting on Moyers' front porch waiting for him.

Tucker followed the President and his group of bodyguards, local Sheriff's officials, and volunteer firefighters into the church. Oddly, no one seemed to mind that Tucker had intruded into the President's group. But then, everyone knew him.

"Mr. President," Clive introduced, "this is Pastor Daily. He graciously opened the doors of the church to those who had been blown out of theirs."

"We have already talked, Pastor." The President smiled and winked an eye. "It's good to meet you in person."

"I'm sorry about that mix-up last night," the pastor said, blushing. "I had no idea."

"I understand," the President assured him. He looked around the Fellowship Hall and smiled at the little ones that were in awe.

When the President came out of the kitchen eating a yeasty, Bismark doughnut, filled with vanilla cream and topped with chocolate icing, Tucker's stomach began to rumble. He stepped farther into the background so the sound could be absorbed by squeaky chairs, happy children, and questions some parents asked about rushed building permits, and if there was a government agency to help those after a disaster. The President told them there was a new agency that was being considered. He called it the Federal Emergency Management Agency (FEMA). However, it would take many more years before it was ready to serve the country. Tucker slipped out ahead of the President's departure.

Over at the Moyer house, Freddie wiggled down on one of the chairs. His feet were stretched out in front of him, and he closed his eyes in the sun. When Tucker finally walked up onto the porch, Freddie explained, "Mom and Dad took Micky home. She said he needed a little slowdown time." He stretched and put his hands behind his head. "I think Mom was right."

Tucker paced back and forth. "The President is finished at the shelter over at the church." The three watched as the head of state reentered his limousine and soon pulled out of the parking lot.

Tucker hoped that the neighborhood would settle down after all the fanfare and hoopla. He liked that safe sameness of his small community.

Goldie stood up and stretched a little. "Now that the security guards have gotten the President out of the area, I think Johnny and I will be able to go home." She reached down and kissed Gramma on top of her head. "Thank you for a wonderful day."

Gramma reached out and took Goldie's hand. "I am so glad you came out today, Goldie. It is always good to see you."

Gramma stretched and held onto the long swing chain to help lift herself up. "I'm going in," she announced. Grandpop and Uncle Jacob joined her.

When they went into the house, that freed up several seats. Christy sat on Gramma's swing, with her eyes closed, and drifted to and fro.

But Tucker paced back and forth on the porch, thinking, worrying, and wishing he had the money to help rebuild homes that weren't anymore. His face was drawn and tight. In fact, he frowned so much, wrinkling his forehead, he started to get a headache.

Tucker stomped his foot and made a decision. He had seen enough that touched his heart. Seeing what the tornado had done to the Klines' lives, wiping out the house and leaving Harvey injured, hurt Tucker, even though it wasn't his own house.

Added to all he had experienced, he also felt badly that he had not checked on his dad earlier. It felt like Sean's home was on the bottom of his list.

Adam and Jacky had made Tucker wish he could bring back a time before the tornadoes hit. Little guys shouldn't experience loss like they had.

But, his decision? One thing was certain, he was not going to feel down or helpless anymore. Tucker flew into action and decided, "I will not be droopy."

Christy opened her eyes. "Droopy?"

"We're going to bring some happiness to the kids over at the shelter." Tucker was excited. The happenings of Palm Sunday would be easier to deal with if the kids had something to create. "What could the kids do first?" It came to Tucker like a lightening bolt. "The sky had turned to an angry black and spilled its twisting clouds all over the neighborhood, pulling up and blowing away everything for some families."

"They can't recreate that," Freddie announced.

"I know." Tucker danced in a circle. "A paper airplane distance flight contest! Let the kids control the stuff that flies in the sky."

Christy opened her eyes and sat up straight. "What are you talking about?"

Tucker bubbled over with excitement. "Let's bring some fun to the kids at the church. And any others that are around. They will be hero pilots, taking to the sky to beat their opponent. I have some stiff drawing paper in my room." He grabbed the front door knob. "I'll be right back."

"Hi, Gramma," he shouted over his shoulder as he tore up the steps to his room. Under a stack of school books he found the large pad of paper. That's all he would need.

Tearing back down the steps, he shrieked, "Christy, Freddie, and I are going over to the church, Gramma." He didn't wait for an answer and darted out the door.

The side street was still covered with large and small pieces of the trash that had been part of a family's home just the morning before. Tucker hated to walk on it. It seemed more like treasures from an Egyptian burial pyramid than trash.

Over in the Fellowship Hall, he plopped the paper down on one of the tables. "Okay, kids. We have a fun activity for you all."

"Me too," Freddie called out.

"And me," Christy added as she went around the tables where families sat and gathered up the children.

Adam and Jacky were sitting together, talking, and pushing each other in fun. Barry Nuemann was there and so was his friend, Linda.

"We're going to have a real airplane flight contest. We'll see whose plane can fly the farthest. We can build them inside, and then go outside so they can take to the air." Tucker pulled over a large chalk board on wheels.

"Okay." He drew an oblong object on the board representing a piece of the paper. "Christy, would you please pass everyone a sheet of paper."

Christy tore off as many pieces of paper as there were children. "Take one and pass it around," she said. Tucker thought she sounded just like Mrs. Hunter.

"Okay," Tucker began again, as he drew a dotted line from the middle of the top of the page to the middle of the bottom. "First, put your name on your paper. Then, fold the paper in half the long way, just like the diagram shows you, and like I demonstrated."

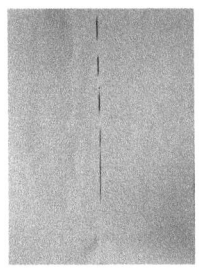
All of the children folded their paper. "There," Adam announced as if he were done with his great Bowing aircraft construction.

"Good work, Adam," Tucker encouraged. "Now, press the fold with your fingernail to hold it tight. Do that with each of your folds."

Tucker watched as the kids tightened up their fold. With the chalk, he drew again. "Now, fold each side again."

Once more, he demonstrated the second fold. "One more time, fold the last piece up as I demonstrated." Everyone folded the paper again and pressed hard like they would if they had an old-fashioned iron in their hand.

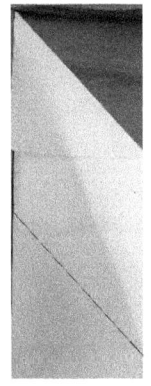

"Now fold for the third time and tighten it up."

"Let's take them outside."

Tucker put his coat on and waited for the children to do the same.

Outside, the air smelled like a touch of rain was creeping in, fresh and clean. The sky gave away the same oncoming rain, but the wind wasn't blowing. Far off to the east, darker clouds were gathering on the horizon. A perfect day to fly a paper airplane.

"Everyone, line up here at the foot of the church steps." Tucker positioned them in a line as the children scattered and shuffled about. "Now, face the parking lot. Let's see how many of you can fly your airplane out past that big oak tree. The winner is the one with the longest flight."

Linda looked up at the sky. The clouds overhead were getting a little gray. "Is it coming back?" she questioned nervously.

Christy tried not to look worried. She went over and gave her a hug. "Linda, your airplane is great, and it can fly during cloudy skies."

Linda smiled and worry seemed to drain from her face. "Thanks."

"Start your engines," Tucker began and demonstrated the position as he lifted his plane to shoulder height. "Now ... FLY!"

Eight paper airplanes, including Freddie's, Cindy's, and Tucker's, flew across the parking lot, like a squadron coming in for a landing. Freddie's plane took a nose dive, crashing about ten feet out from the steps.

"Oh no," he yelled and bent at his knees in helplessness. "I have disappointed my Lieutenant Colonel and shattered my possibility of winning." Freddie peeked out of the corner of his eye and giggled.

The other seven paper jets continued to fly on coarse and swooped to a landing, one at a time. Everyone raced to the landing strip and bent over the farthest plane. Tucker picked up the roaring tiger carefully and unfolded it enough to see the winner.

"Tony!" Tucker shouted. "Which one of you is Tony?"

A boy about Micky's size and age stepped forward. "That's me. I won? Wow," he chattered on. "My dad will be so proud. He was a piolet in the war!"

"Then you're the ace pilot in our squadron, Airman. You deserve the congratulations!" Tucker pulled up Tony's hand and waved it in the air. "The champion! You win …." He had forgotten the prize. Then, excited, he announced, "You win a Hershy's chocolate candy bar."

"Wow," Tony yelled. "I love those!"

The sun had crept behind some incoming clouds, Uncle Jacob called nimbus. They were clouds that formed a thick gray layer of possibility, a possibility of rain.

The kids had experienced enough wet and bad weather. "Grab up your airplane and let's all go inside." He said nothing about the incoming weather change. He just wanted the kids to have the most positive day ever.

Chapter Thirty-Five
SLAPSTICK

Tucker and his friends went home for lunch. He was hungry and couldn't think of anything but food when he was in that state. Even with his stomach growling like a bear, he could still hear himself saying that he was doing some good over at the church.

Before Gramma got lunch on the table, Tucker sat in the corner of the living room and read the chapters of Matthew Mrs. Kline had assigned. Would it make any difference? Maybe there would be no Sunday school on Easter. He shook his head in disbelief. Before she left to take her husband to the hospital, she said, "I'll see you on Sunday." Tucker knew that Mrs. Kline would follow through, if she was able.

This was certainly the time when it would be easy for confusion to set in for Tucker. His week of vacation had been violently blown into the wind. Just as so many houses had been jerked up into the sky, only to crash to the ground.

The "before" was Palm Sunday morning, a great Sunday school class, and a nice afternoon before the wind blew in. He had to believe he was now living in the "between," the heart-breaking time in which everyone had to dig out of the mess after the "happening." In the "between," he had to ask God to walk with him because he didn't know where to go or what to do next.

"God, I don't know what to ask. I just want to walk with you as I try to help people. Amen." It was short. Tucker had to find the words to say what he wanted to say. He didn't want to worry about his next plan. Gramma had always told him that God knows his heart, and he had to depend on that. God knows that Tucker doesn't know himself.

"Lunch is on the table," Gramma called from the dining room.

Tucker could smell the bacon he had bought at Winkler's a few days before. There was a whole platter of it, with pieces of bacon sticking out in all directions. A stack of yeasty bread was on a small plate, beside the huge mess of bacon. Smooth, naturally sweet, homemade applesauce filled small bowls at each place. Gramma had put up the sauce in the fall. Thirty-two glass, pint Ball jars were lined up like tin-soldiers on the pantry shelf in the basement. She was out of milk, so a tall glass of lemon-flavored iced tea stood at each place. The bacon made a tall, tasty sandwich.

Tucker nearly inhaled his meal. Betsy watched with wide eyes. "Where are you going in such a hurry?"

"Back over to the church."

"Why? What are you doing over there?"

Tucker gulped down the last of his tea. A little stream dripped from his chin. He blotted it on a paper napkin and smiled.

Since Gramma was getting older and wanted to cut the number of wash loads, she finally gave in and asked Tucker to buy some of the wasteful paper napkins he had told her about.

Tucker looked at Betsy in disbelief. "I'm helping the kids to forget the bad stuff." He jumped up from the table. "Excuse me." Without waiting, he collected his jacket and darted out the door.

Walking over to the church, he smiled at the rainy afternoon. Micky and Freddie were sitting on the top step of the church. "Well, two Coopers beat me to the door."

Micky jumped up. "I want to help, too."

"What did you have in mind?" Tucker asked and looked at Freddie with a *what's up* look.

"It wasn't me," Freddie denied. "It was my man, Micky. He's the one who came up with this one."

"I thought we could have a Slapstick[8] tournament. Aunt Viola gave me four decks of cards. So, sixteen people can play. The winner at each table would have a play-off to see who the final champion, the winner would be."

Tucker just stared at Micky at first. "That is brilliant." Quietly, to Freddie, Tucker asked, "How does he do it?"

In the church's Fellowship Hall, Tucker could smell the sweet aroma of fresh baked doughnuts. It smelled like Gramma's recipe, but she hadn't baked them in a few years. He knew that the President had eaten a Bismark. He wondered if they had other kinds in the kitchen as well.

"You look faint," Mrs. Daily sympathized. "Would you and the Cooper boys like a doughnut? We baked some more after the President left. They're still warm."

"We came to help. If eating a doughnut would help you, we'd be happy to assist," Tucker teased.

"That would help a lot," Mrs. Daily agreed. "If Tucker McBride says something is good, it is a Blue-Ribbon winner."

There were eleven kids by the afternoon, probably ages six to twelve as far as Tucker could guess. "Good afternoon." Tucker ate a large bite of the pastry and swallowed hard. It was a chocolaty wonder. "How about a Slapstick tournament?"

"What is Slapstick?" one of the girls asked flatly, with her arms folded across her chest.

"It's a card game," Micky smarted back.

Tucker saw weary sadness on her face, not sass. "Micky, she's a little sad. Do you think our game would make her happy?"

Micky put on a big smile. "I laugh a lot when I play Slapstick."

Tucker didn't wait for the girl to get excited about the game. He thought the game itself would do the job. "You're Sissy Shaffer, aren't you?"

She nodded a little but didn't look up. Every few minutes she would sigh deeply.

"I work sometimes at the filling station," Tucker explained. "I pump the gas. Remember the gasoline that you said smelled strong and a little sweet. You come in there with your dad. Is he here?"

"Mom's in the hospital. Dad's there with her. He told me to stay here," she whispered. Her eyes were still focused on the laces in her shoes.

"Okay, Sissy. Let's take up the time until your dad gets back by having some fun." Tucker touched her shoulder, guiding her gently to one of the tables. "Kids," he announced, "we're going to play a game, Slapstick. Let's have four players to a table."

The other kids chose a seat as the groups gathered. That left Sissy at a table by herself. "Barry, you move over here with Sissy, Micky can take Barry's place, Freddie and I will make this table a full four."

They hurried to position themselves. "Playing the game was Micky's idea. He even brought the cards. Let's give Micky a big hand to say, thank you."

Everyone hooted and clapped. Smiles began to cross their lips.

"Okay," Tucker began, "let's go over the rules. Someone at each table deals out all of the cards, face down. The player to the left of the dealer flips out the top card in their pile in the middle of the table. The next player does the same thing. When someone turns up a Jack, all the players race to slap their hand on top of the Jack first. The player who slaps the card first, gets the whole pile of played cards. You keep going until one of the players has gotten the whole deck. If someone slaps a card that isn't a Jack, the mistaken slapper has to give one of his cards to the player whose card they slapped." Some of the players had a blank look on their faces.

"I've never played this slapping game before," Linda said slowly.

Pastor Daily had listened to the instructions and offered to help.

"Tucker, go ahead and start the game," he said as he took one of the decks and shuffled the cards. "One of you at each table, shuffle. You don't have to shuffle like me. You can do it any way you want to. I'll go from table to table to help out until each of you catch on to the rules of the game."

The game began a little slowly, and Tucker wondered if their effort to bring some happiness into the kids afternoon would fail. But, when the first Jack was flipped up, and everyone at the table slapped it, they all bust out laughing. The game speeded up, with laughter and walloping fun, until each group had a winner.

Tucker felt good about the game. But wondered how it really was part of the "between." When he looked at Sissy's smile, he understood. Helping those who are walking through the heart-broken time, to find a little joy for a while, was how he needed to spend the day.

Chapter Thirty-Six
ANOTHER IDEA

The "vacation" week trudged on. It was true, Tucker didn't have school or home work. But it was ... well, different than he expected.

Wednesday afternoon, he worked at the service station so Butch could drive south of Goshen to help get his wife out of the ditch. Tucker overheard when she called back and spoke "loudly" about why he hadn't gotten there yet. She had said something about a deer in the road in her frantic phone call. From Tucker's nearby listening and Butch's later explanation, she told him she had walked over to a nearby house, but the people were Amish, so they didn't have a telephone or a car. They were kind and willing to help, but the father of the house had taken the horse and wagon into town. There was no way to pull her out of her predicament.

Wilhelmina walked over to the house across the street from the Amish family. From there, she was able to call Butch at work.

"You're lucky Tucker has time off," Butch huffed into the phone. He looked down in embarrassment. "I suppose you heard a lot of that. She's a little worried."

Tucker had agreed to come in to cover for Butch's absence. He had been helping with the younger children at the church. Every day, he thought of another game to play or another way to boost their spirits. He liked inspiring the kids to think of the best thoughts. Still, Butch needed him. Or, better said, Butch's wife needed Butch, who needed Tucker.

Everyone who came into the station that afternoon that Tucker worked was droopy. The energy of spring and the expectation of Easter was blown away with the wind a few days before.

"Hi, Tucker," Mr. Justine's son, Jinx, called out the back window as his dad pulled onto the station's drive. "Are you ready for Easter?"

"Nothin' much to get ready," Tucker laughed. "I've been helping a lot at the church this week."

"No Easter egg hunt at your house?" Mr. Justine said with a chuckle.

"No one's young enough to want to hunt eggs at our house." Tucker remembered the eggs Uncle Jacob would hide when he was little. He and Betsy had fun searching everywhere in the big yard. One year, Tucker even checked the root cellar, and a family of opossums scuttled out.

Then Gramma would devil a few of the eggs by cutting them in half, adding mayonnaise, salt, and a dot of mustard. When he was little, he didn't want Gramma to call them Deviled eggs. So, she started calling them summer eggs. Deviled eggs sounded evil to little Tucker.

The rest of the Easter eggs were made into egg salad for lunch time sandwiches. Gramma never let anything go to waste.

Tucker stopped in the middle of the drive with the gas hose in his hand. The distinct, slightly sweet, and pungent odor of gasoline fumes filled the air, just like Sissy described. "That's it!" Strange how a happy memory, visited for a while, could wipe away the sad stuff.

"That's what?" Mr. Justine joked.

"The kids at the church could have an Easter egg hunt," Tucker sputtered, beaming. "We could do it on Easter Sunday just like they were home again."

Mr. Justine tapped the back of the seat, a signal for Jinx to settle his wiggly ways. "Our family could donate some eggs," he said. "But, I thought they hoped to have all of the families placed in temporary homes by Saturday afternoon."

"I forgot that." Tucker finished filling the gas tank and replaced the cap. "I know." Tucker hung the hose back on the gas pump and tapped Jinx's fingers on the open car window in fun. "We could invite all the kids who stayed there this week, to come back on Friday for an Easter egg hunt. It would be a fun day for everyone. I could be right before the Good Friday candle light service."

"Tucker, that's perfect." Mr. Justine slapped two dollars and sixty cents into Tucker's hand for the ten gallons of gasoline he had just pumped. "Something awful happened on Palm Sunday, but you are trying to make this week a blessing for the kids."

Tucker smiled to himself. *A heart-breaking day blew in and blew everything away. Heart-filling days are creeping in already, with a few miracles along with it.*

Chapter Thirty-Seven
AN EGG HUNT

Tucker, Christy, Freddie, and Micky were in charge of hard boiling the eggs. They boiled them in the church kitchen on Thursday afternoon. So the parents could watch the children have fun after all that had happened, the hunt was scheduled for early Friday evening after Mom and Dad got home from work, and before the evening service. Good Friday would be a good Friday. Friday morning, Tucker, Betsy, Christy, Freddie, and Micky, along with Vinny, Gus, and Morty gathered to color them.

"Let's set up an assembly line," Tucker said as he organized the eggs and die in a straight line. "If Henry Ford says that the best way to get the job done is an assembly line, it's good enough for us, too."

Eight bowls of egg die were prepared. The basic colors of red, blue, yellow, green, orange, and pink were mixed. Two additional bowls of yellow and blue were prepared because they were Micky's favorite colors. Tucker depended on Micky to know what the younger kids would like.

"You're the expert here, Micky," Tucker said and laughed as he put a bowl of crystal blue die in front of the five-year-old. "You're closer to their age, so we trust your choice of colors."

Tucker whipped out a sack he had brought from home. He pulled out a piece he had made from a wire coat hanger. It had a loop on one end that extended into a long wire. "I made one for each of us," he announced. "So we don't smudge the colored egg by holding it with our fingers, we put the egg in the loop and dunk it into the die."

"Well, I'll be a kumquat," Vinny said, gapping at the wire.

Micky wrinkled his nose. "I've eaten a kumquat. It's like a sweet little orange. You can eat the whole thing, peeling and all. I like the one I ate."

Tucker stared at the little guy. "Micky, you are a ... I don't know. You surprise me all the time."

Christy watched the color on her first egg darken to a sun-bright yellow the longer she held it under the die. With wide eyes, she laughed. "This is fun, Micky. Tucker, you sure had a good idea this time."

"Thank you, Christy." Tucker dipped his egg up and down in the cherry red die with the wire dipper. "Sometimes, I get a worthy idea."

Gus dipped his first egg into the bowl with green die in front of him, seeming to be mesmerized. "I can't believe it," he whispered. "I've never done anything like this before."

"Your mom didn't color eggs for Easter?" Tucker asked.

"No." Gus was quiet and said very little. Then he added, "Mom said she couldn't afford to waste eggs for coloring."

"But, they aren't wasted," Tucker tried to explain. "Gramma makes all kinds of dishes, and sandwiches with them."

"Mom said, 'No,'" Gus answered. "We don't raise chickens."

"We don't either," Christy agreed.

Tucker changed the subject. "Do you want to sing, 'I Wish I Had a Whisker on the Easter Bunny's Chin?'"

"No!" they all yelled in unison.

Tucker saw that Gus was uncomfortable. But, his attempt to change the subject didn't work. No one wanted to sing his song. But they did begin to talk and laugh as they colored the Easter eggs. Tucker smiled. It was a good between day. And seeing the smiles on the three bullies was truly a miracle.

That evening, twenty-three children from ages ten years old and younger gathered in the Fellowship Hall to hunt for Easter eggs. Each carried an Easter basket, borrowed from the church. They scoured the Lost and Found closet for anything that would pass as a basket. One had a black bowler hat that had been in the closet for years. Several had Christmas gift sacks with handles, that had no gift tag attached. Two of the children each carried one of a pair of children's size, shiny rain boots no one had claimed. Those and other such "found" items were proudly carried by the children.

"Be aware," Tucker announced, "the eggs are not all in this room. You can also hunt on the steps, the upstairs hallway, and check the yard outside."

The children ran around in circles, laughing and bumping into each other. Up the steps, down the steps, inside and outside. Finally, Tucker noticed that they seemed to develop a plan. They flowed like one machine, checking every corner, behind every piece of furniture, and inside every cup or potted plant that could possibly hide an egg. They systematically filled their baskets with brightly colored eggs. Laughing and playing, they gathered in the Fellowship Hall and compared how many each had found. It was a good afternoon, an "after" afternoon.

Chapter Thirty-Eight
EASTER SUNDAY

Tucker and the others in the Sunday school class sat in the church balcony, staring at the stained-glass window on the wall behind the alter. Symbols of Christ and His church, surrounded by yellow glass, glowed back at them.

It had only been a week since they were there on Palm Sunday. The events of that previous Sunday evening still sat heavily on everyone. The week had been tiring, even for those whose home was spared by the tornado. Instead of joking, teasing, and poking each other, they were all worn out and sat quietly. Each wail of the wind, each bent and broken tree, were buried in their long-term memory.

But it's Easter, Tucker thought. Easter is the "miracle-after," when Jesus defied the cross and the agony since he was arrested. He actually rose again to glorify God. Everything that had happened tumbled through Tucker's mind like a bag of spilled marbles, rolling and bouncing into the corners of his memory.

Some days during that previous week, it was hard to know which marble to pick up first. Everything seemed urgent. Tucker had helped everyone, everywhere, in every way he could. Each marble he picked up and put back in its pouch seemed like a small task. Then he thought of the whole week, and a knot formed in his throat.

That Sunday morning, when Birdie Kline came into the second row of balcony pews, Tucker and the others stood and clapped. Christy took a handkerchief from her pocket and blotted some salty tears from her eyes. Since the service hadn't started yet, she hurried over and gave Mrs. Kline a hug. "How is your husband?"

"He's okay," Birdie answered with a grateful smile. "Tucker," she took his hand as he came over to her, "Harvey said to thank you again. You were an answer to prayer."

One little marble was an answer to prayer? Tucker found it hard to grasp the idea. "Did Mr. Kline come today?"

"No," she answered, unwilling to let go of Tucker's hand. "We're staying with my sister and her husband in Goshen, until we find an apartment or somewhere to stay. We hope to remain here in the Dunlap area. But, we know there are probably a lot of other families whose home were damaged or destroyed, who would also like to find something in the area. The school is going to let those children who have to locate outside of the school area to drive in for the rest of the year. Car pools have developed."

"That is great," Tucker said, amazed by the way the entire community was pulling together to make the lives of all those in the path of the tornado work. Another marble picked up.

"And, your husband?" Christy asked again.

Mrs. Kline patted Christy's hand. "Thank you for asking, Christy. Harvey's leg is still swollen a lot, and he's in pain. But, he won't admit it. He decided to stay at Mary Rose's house. Sis and her hubby went to their church in Goshen."

Sharon's chords on the organ soared, announcing the start of service about a man who rose from the grave and went home. Then Gramma's part on the piano rang out, as the two played the first hymn through, before the choir started the processional. Then everyone sang,

> Christ the Lord, is risen today, Alleluia!
> Earth and heaven in chorus say, Alleluia!
> Raise your joys and triumphs high, Alleluia!
> Sing, ye heavens, and earth reply, Alleluia![12]

The choir's processional was beautiful. Thelma Garber usually played the piano while Tucker's cousin Sharon played the organ. Thelma's home was one of the many that were destroyed in the tornado, and Thelma was still in the hospital.

Thelma had just started to run down the basement steps when the house was rattled by the thundering wind. It felt to Thelma that the house had tipped up and dumped everything in the living room toward the basement stairs. All of the furniture, chairs, tables, and lamps slammed toward the steps and pushed her off her feet. She rolled down the treads, shoes over ponytail, and landed on the concrete floor with a broken arm. The pain was terrible.

With Thelma unable to play the piano, Gramma took over the white ivories. Even from the balcony, Tucker could see her small smile. She loved to play music for the congregation. Tucker had heard the words and music of praises to the Lord, since he was a baby. Those precious words were now part of Tucker.

After the service, Tucker and Freddie asked Mrs. Kline at the same time, "Will we have Sunday school?"

"Of course," she said with a turned-up chin. "I'm afraid there are no cookies this week, however. I haven't totally understood my sister's oven yet."

Anna beamed. "Don't worry about that, Mrs. Kline. Mom said you probably had no way to bake. So I helped her make cookies yesterday. I already put them in the classroom."

"Anna, how sweet," Mrs. Kline said, her eyes wide and her smile warm.

The service began with the same choir processional, the greeting, the invitation for prayers, the offering, more hymns, the scripture, and the sermon. Although the world had been jerked off their foundation, risen by the great wind, and slammed to the ground, there was a safe sameness that Easter Sunday morning. Yet, every Sunday there was something new, something for Tucker to take home and chew on for the next week.

After the service, Tucker and the rest of the class hurried into the room with bright yellow walls and a large beige area rug. A huge platter of iced sugar cookies in the shape of Easter eggs and decorated with icing swirls and gold icing rick-rack around the edge sat on a table.

"Everyone," Mrs. Kline announced. "Let's thank Anna for these cookies." She took a bite of the sugary sweetness and covered her mouth to add, "They are delicious, another blessing to add to all the rest."

Anna smiled a happy smile, without a trace of woe. She curtsied deeply. "Thank you. Thank you very much."

Christy clapped her hands. "This is great," she said with a giggle. "Thanks to you and your mom, Anna."

Yvonne bit off a piece of cookie thoughtfully and sat down on one of the chairs that were in a semi-circle. "But, Mrs. Kline, you lost your home in the storm. How is this the blessing time?"

The other members of the class sat quietly, each seeming to try to understand the day. But, Tucker may have listened the most. Yvonne's questions echoed his own.

Mrs. Kline smiled. "I don't design the blessing, Yvonne. God does. My blessing is that Tucker and his dog, Joe, found my Harvey. A nice man named Darren Stuart guided Harvey out of the basement. It was Tucker's brilliant memory of childhood that allowed him to lift himself out of the dark. My sister loved me enough to take us in, and friends, and our insurance company, will rebuild our house. A blessing isn't like placing an order for a Super Prayer Burger from the Hasty Prayer Hut, then we reject God's blessing because He didn't include the piccalilli. A blessing is God's gift. We don't place an order and wait for Him to fulfill it."

Yvonne seemed to need more. Munching thoughtfully on the cookie, she asked, "What if your husband had died?"

Mrs. Kline smiled a knowing smile. "Then his blessing would be in heaven. And mine would be the love of all those who loved him here."

Yvonne continued questioning. "But your house is gone."

Mrs. Kline leaned closer with a hushed voice. "The 'after' will always be different from the 'before.' God always designs the 'after' to make it our blessing and our way of serving Him. He'll reveal the 'how' we serve Him within the little miracles we experience along the way."

Tucker smiled, the kind of smile that shines on the inside. There had been a "before," then the "between," now, with the delicious cookie, he was enjoying the first "heart-filling miracle." He prayed he wouldn't miss any of the small miracles along the way, or fail to find a scattered marble. Anytime there were good friends, and cookies, Tucker's heart was full.

Afterword

Tucker McBride lived in the little village of Dunlap, Indiana. His happenings are based on those of my husband, Bill Rapp, who lived with his grandparents and three siblings in the big white house on the corner.

The Palm Sunday tornadoes did not happen in Tucker's young life. The double headed tornado and the second tornado hit Dunlap on Palm Sunday evening, April 11, 1965. The finger of the tornado went down the street we lived on. I called it Harvest Avenue in the book, but it was Myers Avenue. My husband Bill (Tucker in the books) saw the tornado coming and witnessed it destroy a barn over on the Mishawaka Road on its way.

Bill had gone over to the filling station to get batteries for the flashlights. When he returned, I took Vicki, age 5, Donna, age 3½, and Jimmy, age 10 months, to the basement while Bill went with Mr. Staley (Mr. Stuart) to help.

The President at the time was not named in the book since it is a historical fact. President Lynden Johnson came to Dunlap the next day. He first called the local pastor, Carl Lemna, but Reverend Lemna hung up on him, the President of the United States.

When the President's limousine came into Dunlap, President Johnson did roll down his window and point at a young boy. It was our ten-month-old son James (Jimmy) on his daddy's shoulders, at whom he was pointing.

Yes, cousin Marlyn did spill coffee on the President, and our church was the shelter for those who survived, but whose homes were destroyed.

God walks with us through the tough times. He's there at the Beginning, and continues to guide us through the Between, until we arrive at the After, full of miracles, if we keep our eyes focused on Him.

Glossary

[1] Rapp, Doris Gaines. It's a Good Day. Copyright Doris Gaines Rapp 2026. St. Francis

[2] Peace Prayer of St. Francis of Assisi (Newer Translation) Yale University
https://files-profile.medicine.yale.edu › documents

[3] Weaver, Abraham E. (1916) *A Standard History of Elkhart County.* The American Historical Society. Chicago and New York.

[4]   Kodak Brownie No.2 Model F camera

[5] Vincent van Gogh, *The Sower.* Van Gogh Museum.
https://www.vangoghmuseum.nl›collection

[6] Jennette Threfall (Lyrics). Hosanna, Loud Hosanna. 1873. Gesangbuch der H. W. k. Hofkapelle (Tune). In the public domain.

[7] Rapp, Doris Gaines. 2026. Good Morning Jesus. Copyright 2026 Doris Gaines Rapp.

[8] Scripture taken from the New King James Version®. Copyright © 1982 by Thomas Nelson. Used by permission. All rights reserved.

[9]  Hepplewhite china cabinet

[10] 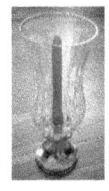 Candle lamp

[11] Paul Huffman. 1965. The *Elkhart Truth* newspaper.

[12] Charles Wesley, 1739 (lyrics) Lyra Davidica, 1708 (music). Christ the Lord Has Risen Today. In the public domain.

Recipes

Orange Jell-O salad[13]

Prep Time: 10 minutes. Additional Time: 30 minutes

Servings: 7

Ingredients:

1 (11 ounce) can mandarin oranges, drained

1 (8 ounce) can crushed pineapple, drained

1 (6 ounce) package orange flavored Jell-O mix

16 ounce cottage cheese

8 ounces frozen whipped topping, thawed

2 tablespoons grated and chopped fine, orange zest

Directions:

Gather all ingredients
Combine oranges, pineapple, and gelatin mix in a mixing bowl. Mix well and chill for 30 minutes.
Add Cottage cheese to the fruit mixture, stir.
Gently fold in whipped topping and lemon zest, chill, and serve.

Lemon Sugar Cookies

Yield: about 24 cookies

Ingredients

Cookies:
- 1 ½ cups white sugar
- 1 cup softened butter
- 2 large eggs
- 2 ¾ cups all-purpose flour
- 2 teaspoons cream of tartar
- 1 teaspoon baking soda
- ¼ teaspoon salt
- ⅓ cup lemon zest

Coating:
- 2 tablespoons white sugar

Directions
1. Gather the ingredients. Preheat the oven to 350 degrees F. Line a baking sheet with parchment paper or lightly grease.
2. With a grater, remove the peeling (the zest) from lemons and grind them fine, enough to make 1/3 cup, depending on a mild lemon flavor or a stronger one.
3. To make the cookies: Beat white sugar, butter, and eggs together in a large bowl using an electric mixer until smooth and creamy. Combine flour, cream of tartar, baking soda, and salt in a separate bowl; stir into creamed butter mixture until dough holds together.

4. To make the coating: Put white sugar on a surface of wax paper or plastic wrap.
5. Shape dough into large, walnut size balls; roll in sugar coating until evenly covered. Arrange balls 2 inches apart on prepared baking sheet.
6. Bake in the preheated oven on the center rack for 12-14 minutes. Cool on baking sheet.

Peppermint Chocolate Chip Cookes

- 1 ⅛ cup flour
- ½ teaspoon baking soda
- ½ teaspoon salt
- ½ cup (1 stick) butter, softened
- 6 tablespoons white sugar
- 6 tablespoons brown sugar
- ½ teaspoon vanilla
- 1 large egg
- 1 cup semi-sweet chocolate morsels
- 2 tablespoons chopped, soft peppermint candy
- ½ cup nuts if desired

375° oven

Combine flour, baking soda, and salt in a small bowl
In large mixing bowl, beat butter, both sugars, and vanilla until creamy
Add egg
Beat in flour mixture slowly
Stir in chocolate, peppermint, and nuts
Use tablespoon and drop onto greased baking sheet
Bake 9-11 minutes until golden brown

Southern Style Green Beans[14]

Put into a pan the amount of fresh, canned, or frozen green beans you need to serve the people expected for dinner.

Add:
Water to cover beans
Salt and pepper to taste
Small pieces of ham (about ¼ cup) or bacon (about three strips, fried or baked crisp and broken into small pieces)
2 tablespoons of finely chopped sweet onion. If you have no fresh onion, you can use onion flakes.
Bring to a boil and reduce heat to barely a bubble.
Cook for 1½ hours, watching that they do not boil dry.

About the Author

Doris Gaines Rapp, PhD, is an author, psychologist, educator, and speaker. This is the sixth book Doris has written about her husband Bill's growing up years in Dunlap, Indiana. She calls them the Tucker books.

As a psychologist, she has counseled with people of all ages. She met with college students during her years directing the counseling center at Taylor University. Then, after their move to the Elkhart area, she counseled with students at Bethel University in Mishawaka. Her experience with people has given her a deep understanding of their emotions, dreams, and disappointments.

Doris and Bill have been married many years, have six children, twelve grandchildren, and soon to enjoy four golden-grans.

Doris enjoys writing her books and hopes you enjoy reading them. Always remember her desire for you: "I hope you live all of your life."

Other Books by Doris Gaines Rapp

Novels:

Lay Your Heart on the Wind

Tucker McBride and the Trumpet Call

Tucker McBride and the Christmas Gift

Tucker's Perfect Day

Tucker McBride's Many Lives

Tucker McBride

A Man of Significance

The Boy with the Golden Horn (A Novel)

The Boy with the Golden Horn – A Picture Book

Escape from the Belfry

Escape from the Shadows

Murder, She Blogged – Just in Time

News at Eleven – A Novel (Prequel to Murder, She Blogged - Just in Time)

Length of Days – The Age of Silence (1st in the trilogy)

Length of Days – Beyond the Valley of the Keepers (2nd in the trilogy)

Length of Days – Search for Freedom (3rd in the trilogy)

Hiawassee – Child of the Meadow

Smoke from Distant Fires

Children's Picture Book:

Shyloe and the Mayor

Lincoln's Christmas Mouse

Collection:

Christmas Feather, one of eight short stories by eight different authors in a collection titled, Christmases Past

Non-Fiction:

Prayer Therapy of Jesus

Promote Yourself

Waiting for Jesus in a Can't Wait World – Advent 2014

Internet Presence

Facebook: facebook.com/doris.gaines.rapp – Author Page

Website: www.dorisgainesrapp.com

www.ingramcontent.com/pod-product-compliance
Ingram Content Group UK Ltd.
Pitfield, Milton Keynes, MK11 3LW, UK
UKHW022237230426
12048UKWH00018BA/1304